Nature

a play

by

DJ Davies

TSL Drama

Dedication

For my parents
Qi

My thanks to my cousin Steph for her patience, and keen pragmatic eye, along with her husband Andy.

Characters
[in order of speaking]

Billy, *a man of 70.*
Fay, *a woman of 26.*
Freddie, *Fay's twin brother.*
Dido, *a dog.*
Banjo, *Billy's brother* [*voice only*].

Huntsman, *wild and domestic animals* [*sounds only*].

A car: *the Messerschmitt* HKR 200, *is silent running.*

3 areas of play:
A Lady's Private Room in rococo style
A Country Road
The Wood

Spring
Night
Present Time

The Room.

Billy, **Fay**

A lady's private room in the rococo style. The principal furnishings are a table, a couch and a chair. A confusion of fruits, cakes and flowers jostle together on the table, against a small silver bell. The room is windowless, sealed and candlelit.
Billy *and* **Fay** *are in full evening wear.* **Fay** *lies asleep on the couch. While* **Billy** *stands beside the chair watching her. He sports a canary yellow bow-tie, perched in a fly-collar above a canary yellow flower in the lapel.*
Brief tableau.

Billy:	[*Whispered*] Lovely. I can almost hear it dream.
	[*He hesitates, approaches and leans over her sniffing at the air with great satisfaction. He hovers, steps backwards and returns to the chair. He hesitates and sits down.*]
	[*Awe*] I could almost taste it. It's gorgeous. It's a work of art. No bruises, no broken bones … it's, it's just like alabaster … as if it's been preserved in a dark room for ages and ages … yeah. Just like Lizzie. [*Beat.* **Fay** *mumbles*] She stirs, she moves! [**Fay** *mumbles*] What? [**Fay** *mumbles*] What?
	[**Fay**'s *eyelids flicker open. She stares ahead.*]
	[*Pleasantly*] Hello Fay. I only have to ring that little –
Fay:	Where …? Who …? [*2 beats*] I, I … Where –?
	[**Fay** *starts. Pause. She sits bolt upright. 2 beats*]
	Am I hurt? Have I been in an accident …? Am I ill? Am I ill?
Billy:	[*Gently*] No, no. Not at all. You're a lovely beautiful

young woman ...

Fay: W-What?

Billy: A glass of champagne, perhaps?

Fay: ... Champagne?

Billy: Yeah. Like an aperitif before dinner. I only have too –

Fay: Dinner?

Billy: Yeah.

[*Silence*]

Fay: [*Suddenly focused*] Where am I? And who are you?

Billy: It's evening Fay. Evening. And you've just missed a lovely sunset. It disappeared real slow over our bluebell wood. It was all sparkly and lovely ... and like it was just made for you.

Fay: Where am I! And who are you?

Billy: ... Of course, it's too dark now.

Fay: [*Abruptly*] Who are you?

Billy: Billy. Billy Bricks?

[*Silence*]

Fay: [*Sharply*] What has happened to me? [*Beat*] Am I hurt?

Billy: What?

Fay: What has happened to me!

Billy: Nothing.

[*Pause*]

Fay: [*Checking her body in a confused manner*] Have you touched me?

Billy: What?

Fay: Have you touched me?

Billy: No!

Fay: But … my body … it feels –

Billy: [*Amazed*] Certainly not! No bloody way! No, no, no! Not a hair, not a stitch, not even a zip! Not me! No! [*Beat*] Not I! [*Beat*] Not ever …!

Fay: But, but my body … it feels –

Billy: No! [*Angry*] No fucking way! [*Beat*] Excuse me. I gave strict instructions not to go beyond your underwear.

[*Silence*]

Fay: Am I hurt? Have I been in an accident – my car! My little car!

Billy: Listen. You're a healthy young woman. And your little car is as good as gold … believe me –

Fay: The Park! My dog! M-My Dido!

Billy: Now calm down. Now don't you worry about anything, everything is going to be alright. They took good care –

Fay: They! They! W-Who are they?

Billy: Listen. They left –

Fay: They? They?

Billy: Calmly now. Yes. They left it tied up to a tree. Near where you and Freddie –

Fay: Freddie!

Billy: Yeah. Near where you and Freddie picnic in Kensington Gardens on a nice summer day.

Fay: Freddie?

Billy: Yeah. On nice days beside The Pond. And I reckon it's probably been home for a few hours now. And I reckon it's tucked into a nice bowl of Pedigree Fido, and having a nice kip in its big basket –

[**Fay** *jumps up and stands unsteadily.*]

Fay: It is she! It is she! She is Dido –!

Billy: [*Commanding*] Sit!

[**Fay** *sits.*]

Billy: Excuse me. [*Gently*] She – Dido is most probably all tucked up and quite safe right now. In fact, she's probably having a nice doggy dream, all about a big bone … at this very minute.

Fay: [*Abruptly*] My Freddie!

Billy: Yeah. That spot where you and him and her …

Fay: My brother Freddie?

Billy: Who else? And right beside your favourite tree. All safe and sound.

[*Silence*]

Fay: [*Studies her clothing*] What's this? Why am I wearing this dress?

Billy: It's the dress you wore at the Serpentine Summer Party last year.

Fay: I know what it is – I bought it! How – why am I wearing it?

Billy: Well –

Fay: You've molested me –!

Billy: No! Nobody's been beyond your underwear – I promise!

[*Pause*]

Fay: Is this abduction? Is this kidnap? [*Beat*] Ransom? Is it ransom? Because if it is my brother and I have very little actual funds … my Father –

Billy: Not at all! I had a dog once. I'm a dog lover. I'm a doggy person, too.

Fay: Why am I here?

Billy: We called him Gort because he only had one eye. [**Fay** *goes to speak*] And he was always banging into artificial objects, like lampposts and railings and even the occasional door. [*A confidential tone*] And I'll tell you something else … he used to purposely piss over a particular style of gentleman's shoe. [**Fay** *shows an abrupt curiosity*] Right! And that it was like a psychological complex – like, like a phobia. And I always reckoned he'd been kicked up the arse a few times by that same style of shoe. Anyway, who's to know –? Just like the time we was standing at the bus stop at the top of our road alongside this gentleman in bowler hat and brolly. And well I looked down into Gort's eyeball and I just knew right there and then that, that gentleman's shoe was giving Gort major grief. Anyway, we're standing at this bus stop at the top of our road, when all of a sudden, I hears the regular hiss and splash … well. The gentleman he looks down at his nice shiny shoe, and then he looks out at the passing traffic all hostile like. [*Beat*] And then this gentleman he looks down at me and then right down at Gort, and then right up into the sky … well. And then he the gentleman he steps very carefully away from the curb. [*Beat*] Anyway, 10 or 11 seconds later we're still standing at the bus stop at the top of our road when I hears the old hiss and splash again … well. The gentleman in the bowler hat and brolly like glares out at the passing traffic. And I glare out at the passing traffic, too. And then he the gentleman he looks right up at the sky all quizzical like. And I do the same too. And we both watched this fluffy little cloud shuffling along and minding its own business. And then he – the gentleman, he looks right up and down the street. And then I look up and down the street, too. And then this gentleman – he looks right down at me, and then right down at Gort all scrutinizing and suspicious like. And I look right up at him all uppity serious and indignant and kinda upset, too. [*Beat*] And then he, the gentleman he looks down at his nice shiny shoe, and then right up at me again. And then right down at Gort ... and well Gort's looking up all sweet and innocent, like. And then this gentleman, he looks right up at the sky again all deep and questioning and philosophical. And me and Gort look right up at the sky all deep and questioning, too. [*Beat*] And then – well, after that we all settled down and sorta stared out at the passing traffic, until the gentleman – he, he all of a sudden steps away from Gort and unfurls his umbrella and holds it up all dainty – just like a Geisha ... and well me and Gort are just left looking at one another – and Gort, well Gort's looking up and grinning at me, and I'm –

[*A deep slightly muffled animal cry – abrupt silence.*]

Fay: What –!

[*A bellow followed by a long series of grunts, and bubbly water sounds – abrupt silence.*]

Fay: What – what is it –!

Billy: Now calm down. Calmly does it. That was just Mike showing off. Mike and Mable my pet hippos.

[*Pause*]

Fay: Who are you?

Billy: I told you. I'm Billy Bricks ... a friend of Lizzie's.

[*Pause*]

Fay: Lizzie?

Billy: Yeah. Your Ma –

Fay: My Mother!

Billy: Yeah. What's with the name?

[*2 beats*]

Fay: What ...? Who –?

Billy: Who?

Fay: Who!

Billy: Oh! The dog. Your dog?

Fay: [*Abruptly*] Dido! Dido!

[*Beat*]

Billy: What's Dido? What like the singer?

[*2 beats*]

Fay: [*With scorn*] Like. Aeneas and Dido.

[*Beat*]

Billy: What like Sony and Cher? [**Fay** *is silent*] Mind you he could smell Ma's cooking from miles away –

Fay: Who?

Billy: What –?

Fay: Who?

Billy: What –? Oh. My dog.

Fay: [*Toneless*] Your dog.

Billy: Yeah. That's right. We grew up together in East Dulwich – not Peckham. East Dulwich. He could smell Ma's cooking from miles away ... she'd make a stew last all week my Ma ... she would.

Fay: Am I a prisoner here?

[*Beat*]

Billy: [*Amazed*] You're my guest!

Fay: So if I chose to leave I can?

Billy: Why would you want to leave? You've only just
arrived … and there's a lovely dinner later on – in fact
I only have to ring that little –

Fay: Dinner here? [*Beat*] Here –!

[*A hippo bellows. The hippos' duet to silence.*]

Billy: That's my Mike and Mable, alright! Mike must've
heard you mention dinner. We can go upstairs later
on and take a peep at my two beauties, if you like?
I've got a big pair of binoculars up there fitted with a
night-sight. And it's got the best view over our little
lake, too. I sometimes like to go upstairs at this hour
in the evening especially on a nice spring night, like
tonight. And just watch them settling down all calm
and peaceful, like. And then sometimes I like to go
down to the lake itself and just twiddle my toes in the
water and just watch my Mike and Mable simply
splashing about and sorta looking at me with their
great big gormless faces. And at other times under a
big yellow moon I'd sit and watch my two darlings
simply snoring away quietly all cuddled up together,
and all just happy, like. [**Fay** *goes to speak*] And at
other times I'd just watch Mable standing there in the
water just watching me with her little piggy eyes, and
flicking her funny little ears all over the place. And
Mike. Well Mike, he's a randy old sod. Do you know I
once watched him watching a slow drifting cloud
drifting right in front of the moon and him getting all
excited about it for ages and ages? He watched that
cloud and Mable just watched me … like all starry
eyed. And I reckon that, that cloud must've looked a
bit like a female hippo, because Mike got that excited

– in fact transfixed. Anyway, after that I'd go take a stroll and visit my Terry –

Fay: [*Nervously*] What is Terry?

Billy: Yeah, Terry. Terry the tiger.

Fay: Oh! Yours … this place – it's a wildlife park.

Billy: Certainly not! These gardens was inspired by Gertrude Jackal.

Fay: [*A corrective tone*] Jekyll, actually.

         [*Beat*]

Billy: Jackal!

         [*Beat*]

Fay: [*Quietly*] Jekyll.

         [*Beat*]

Billy: Jackal?

         [*2 beats*]

Fay: [*Steely*] Jekyll.

         [*Silence*]

Billy: [*Patiently*] Jackal, Jekyll! [*Upbeat, and referring to the room*] Anyway, do you like it? It's not real. I found it in a furniture book and I thought it'd be nice and feminine to wake up too. [*Admiring the room*] Some associates of mine know about such things and put it together for me. It's not real. It's French.

         [*Beat*]

Fay: What is real?

Billy: Well. You're actually sitting in a room in a castle I acquired a few years ago. And outside this little room it's all pointy windows and twisty spires. It's really lovely. It belonged to the great, great grandson of the original owner. The young man even had his own personal motto chiselled over the door. [*Abrupt, focused and awkwardly pronounced*] 'Papaveris ultra perfudit arva iacent in O' blivone.'

[*Beat*]

Fay: [*With indifference*] 'Beyond … beyond lie poppies drenched in oblivion.'

Billy: [*Impishly*] Mystical, right?

Fay: [*Dismissive*] Poppies poached from Virgil, I'd say.

Billy: Er?

Fay: It's like something my brother would dream up.

Billy: Er, yeah? [*Beat*] Well, it's a nice little place with a nice little wood, in a nice little valley. It's a funny place too, with its very own easy-going climate. Yep. Living is pretty easy going down here in consideration of the balls up going on elsewhere. Even the wind itself settles down nicely in the sun in the morning, and behaves itself right round the clock. And the snows seem to stay in the hills, and never really settles on the valley floor. And anyway, don't bother us really. And our flowers and shrubs – all lovely little fellas in fancy hats, are all puffed up mostly all year round. And we got tropicals here, too. I mean like red and blue parrots, who fly in and out of the trees, and talk a lot, and don't ever seem to wanna go home – it's that nice here … yeah. Welcome to Ambrosia. And our lake is fed by a river that comes out of a cave, the locals call The Devil's Door – right! And it's full of jumbled bones and stuff, and drawings of deer, wolf and bison on its walls, too. That's according to Banjo, that is.

Fay: Banjo?

Billy: My brother Banjo. And he reckons the locals told him – folklore, that is. That the valley sometimes every now and again sorta closes down, sorta shuts up shop, so to speak. Because they reckon the valley is conscious and living, and a bit like a nervous system. And every now and then in dodgy times, it decides to close down for a while. They call it The Sleep. I personally reckon it's a con to get the odd pint out of the odd tourist in The Kingfisher.

Fay: [*Intrigued*] You mean animism?

Billy: Well. [*Beat*] If by that you mean like a toad talking to a tree … well, yes, I suppose so. This valley was actually carved out by a slow-moving glacier about 20,000 years ago during the last great ice age, that's according to my brother Banjo. [*Thinking out loud*] He's coming from a really weird place at the moment … [*to* **Fay**] he just camps out between the wood and the village … I don't know what to make of it? [*2 beats*] Anyway I sometimes go along to see my Terry. In fact, we spend quite a lot of time together, now that Banjo's not about a lot. I just sit there watching him, watching me with his big yellow eyes. And then I just sorta start talking to him like a real long-time buddy … yeah. But what really gives me the goose pimples is when one of the lads dangles a nice fat rat right over Terry's nose … and I watch it wiggle and get all excited, as Terry, Terry grins and bears his big beautiful teeth … just like Gort used too.

Fay: Is, is it safe?

Billy: Well? Right about now he's just waking up. [*Beat*] People laugh. I know. I hear them. But if St Frankie can talk to the Big Bad Wolf, then why can't I talk to my Terry? I hear them … the others. I know. They laugh. You tell me?

Fay: [*Agreeably*] Of course, of course ... and there's a village?

Billy: [*Toneless*] Yes. [*Beat*] There's a village. And we have a pub, a post shop and a policeman.

Fay: Really!

Billy: Of course. We're just outside Tunbridge Wells.

Fay: [*Visibly relaxing*] And the village. Is it far?

[*Pause*]

Billy: It's part of my domain.

Fay: You own it? The village?

Billy: The village, the valley, lock stock and barrel.

Fay: So, the village must work for you.

[*2 beats*]

Billy: Yes and no. They're a funny lot. It's like they've all slept in the same bed for about 200 years, like they've all tumbled out of the same bum – ya' know, red hair, three freckles and a hairy mole under the nose.

Fay: Really ... oh dear!

Billy: Fay.

Fay: Yes?

Billy: That's a really lovely name ...

Fay: Thank you. Perhaps after dinner we might go for a walk, and have a pint in the pub?

Billy: [*Abruptly*] No. Not tonight. They're a funny lot. Fun and games tonight. I allow them the use of the wood 2 or 3 times a year. They're a religious folk. They're into nature, and worship a particular tree in our bluebell wood. [*With irony*] 'If you go down into the woods tonight you'll definitely get a surprise.' You might fancy a walk to smell our nice flowers, or, perhaps you might prefer to go watch Mike and Mable settle down for the night. Or, let's say you decide to take a nice moonlit stroll down a particular delightful primrose path. Okay. But as you approach – say, a nice big rhododendron bush you hears a rustle and a grunt … and all of a sudden from out of the bush jumps this big naked fella all painted up with the sun and the moon tattooed on his arse, and spitting and bearing his big yellow teeth … [*Warmly*] just like Terry. [*Darkly*] No. [*Abruptly*] Turnips. No, no. You're better off here tonight. A nice organic pear, perhaps?

[*2 beats*]

Fay: No thank you.

[*Beat*]

Billy: A nice slice of angel cake, then? [*Beat*] With a cup of tea, to wet the whistle?

[*2 beats*]

Fay: No thank you.

Billy: Low calorie. Not that you need to watch the weight, though …

[*Pause*]

Fay: No thank you.

[*Beat*]

Billy: It's no bother …

[*2 beats*]

Fay: No thank you.

Billy: Sure? [*2 beats*] What about a nice cheese and pickle sandwich, then? [*2 beats*] Just to get the juices going?

[*Silence*]

Billy: Well, well, well … it's a long way from Ma's little shaking house beside the railway track. And that little house seemed to have its very own particular idea about climate change long before climate change became fashionable. It actually had its own weather system between the attic and the cellar … and the very idea of a snowball fight in the attic in August was not at all unrealistic. Especially when the old Siberian, the old white tiger, came a'calling. [*Beat*] And what with its rattling windows, peeling walls and wailing pipes, together with the daily assault of big black rats in waves up against the kitchen table all day and all night, along with generous amounts of soot, smoke and shit, and well our poor Ma she used to pretend the rats came over on the ferry from Belgium for the day – like outa Walt Disney all chuckles and furry little faces. [*Beat*] I mean amongst the smoke and smells you'd climb the stairs and offer up a Hindu prayer beneath its trembling ceiling especially during the rush hour. And what with its yard all overgrown with nettles peeping in the windows and pushing up through the wooden floor, and up the stairs – ah! But that was before Goggle … [**Fay** *shows a reluctant curiosity*] yeah. Goggle. Our goat Goggle. [*Musing*] Funny. But back then I thought all goats were vegetarian. Anyway, our little house operated on a policy of round the clock survival. And a busy and thriving little place it was, too. There were lots of comings and goings, like Shakespeare by moonlight. Because we operated in a black-market economy in those days. Which was very much the fruits of a post-war system … secrets and whispers and footsteps in the fog. And we were organized and really driven, with every corner and piece of furniture piled high with tins of food, frocks, shoes, suits and such – in fact anything we could get our hands on. Yes. Our little house was a veritable Aladdin's Cave. A business associate of mine reckons … 'We were a happy fusion of exponential happenings in the transportation of merchandise 24/7.' And went on to say. 'We were the apogee of human survival.' He reckons. And so, Ma, and us kids we all slept in one big bed, and sat on one big bumpy armchair. And I can tell you the nights in our little bedroom were highly musical indeed, with Gort and Goggle all cuddled up together on the floor, and adding significantly to the atmospheric entertainment. And Ma, Ma she sleepily would say, 'Go on then, go on. Open the window and let the moon in, but remember to ask her nicely if she'd hypnotize the goat.' Because Goggle, Goggle … well, Goggle [*Deadpan*] he played the trombone. Ya' know I do believe Gort really adored Goggle, because he'd always bump into him in a really affectionate way – amazing really! An' yeah, Ma, she used to scrub his arse with lavender water, to hygienise the air. But just sometimes I liked to be alone, and think about Ma, myself and my future. So, I'd go up and lie on the roof all alone, and allow a baby squirrel to come along and nibble at my big toe to test the power of my concentration … [**Fay** *goes to speak*] and as I said, I'd lie back and think about Ma and business and Dad the legend, who went away to war, and died of the atomic disease in Australia. [*Beat*] And at other times I'd just sit and watch Goggle peacefully chewing away on a nettle, or a dandelion flower down below in the backyard. Ah! But that was before the psycho pigeon arrived. It came one Saturday morning straight out of a clear blue sky. And it actually struck at precisely 10.00 a.m. I know because like Joshua I could see exactly where the sun stood still at that particular hour. And anyway, I knew the time alright, because I could hear the local church banging in a wedding. And this pigeon had swooped right down and dug its talons into poor Goggle's back, and then spewed and shit all over him, too – yeah! Before it disappeared out into the wide blue yonder, again. And this rather odd behaviour actually happened for three Saturdays on the trot, at precisely the same hour. True. Well, I was intrigued by this pigeon's behaviour. And for the first time in my life I wasn't just thinking about business, and Ma and such, but higher things like knowledge and wisdom, too. So, I decided to go along to Dulwich Park and seek out a birdman. Well, I found a group of nice gentlemen down by the lake. And so, I gingerly approached one gent in particular – you know with a kind of anticipated excitement, like this was the first real serious event in my life. Anyway, I looked at the nice gentleman and informed him in some detail about Goggle and this psycho pigeon. Well. The nice gentleman he looked down at me over his big binoculars and sort of scrutinized me for a while. And then he looks out over the lake and kinda studies a couple of ducks bobbing up and down for a few minutes. And then he, the gentleman, he looks right up and studies the tree right above my head. And then after a while he, he looks down at me over his big binoculars again, and sorta scrutinized my face for a bit. [2 beats] And then the gentleman, the expert, the birdman ... [A look of total bewilderment] he tells me to fuck off? [Beat] The expert, the birdman, the gentleman ...? I felt that biffed and baffled after that, that I didn't wanna bird watch not for years and years, not until I bought my own pair of binoculars … I was that upset! [*Sheepishly*] And like sometimes I get a crocodile in me top hat – like, like all snappy and nasty, like. And so, I got home and told my brother Banjo, and me and him went back – and well … we kinda stoned a few swans. [*Silence*] It wasn't nice and it should've not happened. And I reckon you're really the first real person I've ever really told. And really silly really, but I've had bad dreams ever since like, like the same feeling I get when I'm sleep walking all invisible up Ma's stairs and round Ma's bed and right up to Ma's roof … all gone and ghostly now but still there, and perhaps a little like the village people who reckon they become invisible every now and again in The Sleep, that is … regret, right Fay? [*Silence. Upbeat*] Yeah. My brother Banjo my best friend. Ma called him Banjo because Ma told us, as she *always* told us, a Doc told her, Banjo was a genius … like a weirdly high IQ like Batman or the Joker, or, or Albert Einstein, – or, or someone. [*Beat*] And I've often wondered whether if it had happened because as a kid he fell through thin ice in Ruskin Park? So, she called him Banjo because she said he was a musical genius. She even bought him an old pub piano and told us he was going to be the biggest singer in the world. [*Beat*] It didn't much matter to us kids, because we already knew he had 2 of the biggest puffed-up lungs in Peckham, and we all reckoned his Father was the singin' n' dancin' Jamaican milk man … my buddy, my best friend, my brother Banjo. People even began to call us *Billy the Kid* – right. Anyway, as if that bird stuff wasn't enough to put up with, in those days in the afternoons Ma and us kids would sit and watch *Children's Hour* together. And all seven of us would bundle onto Ma's lap all nice and comfy and springy because Ma was O'beast long before it became topical, and of course Gort would spread out on a lovely piece of carpet sleepy but alert for the odd chip, or the occasional lobbed gobstopper. [*Mumbling*] Yeah, unfortunately, Ma, she was never shy around a nice pork chop. Anyway, on another, rather trying day Ma and all us kids was watching Bill and Ben on the telly, when all of a sudden Ma turns and stares at me all peculiar and dramatic ... and she says in a really spooky voice ... 'I'm gonna call you Bill' – like I was The Wild Boy who'd just walked outa the Borneo jungle ... right! Anyway a few days after that the goat wandered into the kitchen from off the back of a van. He just stood there with his nose resting on the kitchen table all peaceful, like. While us kids all stood about eating bread and jam ... Goggle. I know, I know ... nostalgia, right, Fay?

[*2 beats*]

Fay: Courtesy is the cornerstone of civilisation. Civilized behaviour will always puzzle the peasant, and, may even intrigue, confuse and disarm the vulgar, the voracious, and the cruel.

[*Silence*]

Billy: Er, well, well – er, yes of course. Thank you, Fay. [*Beat*] Fancy a banana?

[*Beat*]

Fay: No.

Billy: Sure?

[*Beat*]

Fay: No.

[*Beat*]

Billy: A few grapes then … organic?

Fay: [*Firmly*] No thank you. [*Beat*] Do the villagers keep house for you?

[*2 beats*]

Billy: Yes and no. No, because when we first came here we popped down into its cellar, and to our complete and utter amazement we found a big boy's chemistry set down there all fitted up and ready to go. [*With irony*] It was quite poetic, really. So, I sent a few of the locals down to tidy the place up a bit. And comes breakfast, dinner and tea and they still hadn't come up. So, I sent one of the boys down to see what was going on. Well, he comes up all breathless and blowy, and tells us, they're all down there all over the floor, and lying about like hippies at a hippy convention, some mumbling in tongues, while others were buzzing like bees, and rolling around all over the bloody floor. [*Impishly*] Yes. It was quite poetic, a bit like your Virgil. [*Beat*] And yes. Because our Willy Wonka work force does keep the gardens and wood nice and clean – but never ever in domestic hygienic areas. [*Impulsively*] you could chew on a chunk of pineapple, right outa my earhole – and no need for a fruit fork either. I'm that *hygienic*. They're a funny lot. When we first arrived here they cordially invited all of us to meet the folks down at The Kingfisher … well, when we gets down there we peeps inside the door and we got a right surprise. Because what we saw was all these turnips all over the place jumping up and down, and like leaping and reeling this way and that right up in the air, that we thought that at any minute they were gonna bounce right out the door and into the bubbling weir. [*Beat*] Absolutely! One of the boys reckoned it was a punk party. But Banjo he said it was definitely tribal. And he should know because ever since we've been down here, all he does is bang on about 'The Motherland'. And he reckons ever since we've been down here, he's been slowly going back to his roots. Banjo, my brother, my buddy, my best friend ... but I don't understand where he's coming from anymore. And he's also started talking up in that funny Jamaican lingo. And he's grown his hair long and wild and dyed it red, yellow and green, and plaited it up tight into knots with gold and silver thread, and hung with tiny emeralds, diamonds and pearls, with two ivory thunder bolts through the top and finished it all of by painting his fingernails black – and started going about calling himself Bo, after some African Thunder god? And reckons he's gonna return to the purity of his gene pool, and keep it nice and clean like the village people do. [*Beat*]. I'd hate to think what Ma would make of it. [*Beat*] Ma, Ma would get really aerated. [*Beat*]. Yeah. He's become a great favourite in the village, a regular Piped Piper, and I don't see much of him now. As I said he lives between the wood and the village ... I don't know what's going on inside his head? And they're a funny lot. And this is a funny place. They reckon that this castle was built on the site of a big manor house that burned down 300 years ago. And listen to this as a piece of historical description. They reckon it belonged to a particular Sir Cecil, who had a big thing about a particular horse. And that the whole house was turned into a temple dedicated to this horse. A horse called Persephone. Even the great fire place, in the great hall he had modelled on the shape of Persephone's backside. Plus, all the tables and chairs, right down to the silver cups and bowls all had her head and hoofs about them. And that his habit every night at precisely 8 o'clock was to ride the horse between livered servants holding up candelabra in the great hall, right up the great staircase and right up to his bed chamber … well, on this particular night while he and the horse were trotting up the stairs, it's reckoned that a piece of hot wax fell onto a powdered wig … well. Up went the stair, up went the horse and up went Sir Cecil with it. And listen to this. It was historically observed that because of the intense heat, all the flowers in all the flower beds opened up and turned up and stared up, along with all the birds, bees and butterflies, and all the rest of the local wildlife in the garden. In fact, they all came up and came out and stood up and stared up as the big house became all papery and transparent. [*2 beats*] And listen to this. It was also historically observed that over 2,000 bottles of French champagne popped in one big bang that blew the roof, the horse and Sir Cecil right up into the air – phew! True. And that it was also historically observed that both horse and rider were last seen flying over a big yellow moon with flames shooting out of the horse's arse. [*A confidential tone*] And that's why the locals think it was a mechanical horse.

[**Billy** *stands up and points in a dramatic fashion at a spot on the floor.*]

[*Whispered*] Here. Right here. It has been historically observed that in a particular season, at a particular hour, and under the influence of a particular moon, Sir Cecil has been seen to trot up the ghostly –

[*A phone rings loudly somewhere in the room. Its ringtone: The Last Strip, from* Gypsy. **Fay** *is startled and jumps up, while* **Billy** *in great embarrassment frantically searches high and low for the phone. He finally locates it on the table in the fruit bowl, spilling the fruit into the room. Into phone, whilst kicking the fruit in anger from under his feet,* **Billy** *gently directs* **Fay** *to sit. She does so reluctantly.*]

Yesss! [**Billy** *listens intently, beaming at* **Fay**. *Into phone*] Right! Right! [*To* **Fay**] Freddie's coming! Freddie's coming to dinner! [*Into phone*] Right, right – fantastic! [*To* **Fay**] And he's got the dog with him! [**Fay** *is visibly animated. He listens. Into phone*] Good! Great – cheers!

[**Billy** *places the phone in his pocket and returns to the chair and sits down.*]

That was my brother Banjo. He'd just now got word from a couple of the boys in town, who spotted Freddie leaving The Crescent –

Fay:	The Crescent!
Billy:	Yeah. In that funny car you've got –
Fay:	Hermann! [*Quietly*] Hermann.
Billy:	Right. And the dog's there, too.
	[*2 beats*]
Fay:	Dido! Dido!
Billy:	Yeah. And the dog is sitting right up there behind him with her paws on his shoulder, and her head sticking out the top, and wearing a pair of goggles all proud and serious, just like a German fighter pilot –
Fay:	Oh Dido!

Billy: [*Watches* **Fay**] Hermann the German, right? [*2 beats*] Howzat! They actually left town over two hours ago, so, given the Friday night traffic, I reckon they should be passing the twinkling lights of Tunbridge Wells about now ... I reckon.

[*Pause*]

Fay: [*Quietly*] Thank you, Mr Bricks.

Billy: [*Settling into the chair*] Relaxavous. Call me Billy. And may I apologize for the way that this whole shambolic business has been handled. It was supposed to have been the beginning of a big birthday party for you both. And Freddie was supposed to be here when you woke up ... Freddie, Freddie, Freddie, he'd be late for his own funeral.

Fay: My brother is reckless, Mr Bricks. But I'm afraid Freddie and I will be spending our birthday with our Father at his nursing home in East Grinstead.

Billy: No worries. It's all been sorted. I've hired a helicopter with two nurses to fly the old gentleman in tomorrow. All safe and sound. Plus. We'll bus family and friends in VIP style all the way. I left all the organizing to Freddie. And I do believe he chose a close friend of yours, a party planner. A young lady called ... Arabella?

Fay: Arabella!

Billy: That's right. Arabella. And a very nice young lady, too. This is a fantastic place! What with the castle and other things. And Arabella is gonna put up a big marquee, with suitable music in Miss *Jekyll's* garden. Plus. A lot of big bouncy things for the kids – they'll love it! [*Beat*] Howzat!

Fay: I'm, I'm quite overwhelmed, Mr Bricks. But I'm afraid my brother is careless and fanciful.

Billy: But it was my idea! Mine. Not Freddie's. I just let him run with it. It's going to be fantastic! And good for the old chap, too.

Fay: But Mr Bricks –

Billy: Not at all! It gives me great pleasure. And I know you've both had a rather difficult financial time of late. And besides Freddie's a dear friend. [*Beat*] And I'd like to be your friend, too … if allowed. So, relax*a*vous.

Fay: [*Reluctantly*] Thank you. But where exactly are we?

Billy: [*Abrupt, focused: he stares beyond her*] 'Dear Mr Bricks, we was happy to hear about you and was just wanting you to know how much we think about your good works in keeping faith and trying to keep up a good green effort in your building trade. Your watchword: Pocket, Planet, Pride, fills us with real hope in you. So, we thought you might help a small rural community of good hard-working folk in trouble, in need of a good caretaker. We wonder would you fancy being the Lord of the Manor? Well, if so, it's a fairy tale castle in its very own valley with its very own lake full of fat jumping fish. The castle was built in 1905 by a Mr Giles Gibert Scott somebody for a Tex T. Ritter II, on the site of an old manor house. It was all decorated up to date with all the modern comforts in 2006, by the great, great, great nephew of Mr Ritter. A Mr Jor – El, a musician by trade was what we was told. We believe he walked off one-night time, and got lost some seven seasons ago, and was never seen again. We miss him here. A nice man. Since then we've gone on and kept the gardens and wood up to scratch, and looking just lovely. It also has the old boat house and gate house, too. And we believe you'd be very happy here. And it's only a few modern miles from the hotel where we think you, you … you …' [*the valley speaks: a beautiful voice*]:

> Softly round the sleeping bees, to the
> Toll of the bell in the solar shadow of the
> Waiting tomb, towards the tree, the tree …
> the tree …

[**Billy** *falls back into the chair.*

Silence]

Fay: [*To herself*] Extraordinary!

Billy: [*He sits up. Normal voice*] I suppose you've realized I'm a mnemonic.

[*Pause*]

Fay: [*Intrigued*] Yes, yes of course. How curious, how clever of you. And poetic, too.

Billy: What?

Fay: A poet too, Mr Bricks.

Billy: [*Puzzled and delighted*] Er – well. It's a bit jumbled up perhaps, but it's pretty precise all the same. Yes, some of my admirers to do with my Earth Awareness Programme. I like helping people, that's all. Especially now the Old Girl has started to shake her shoulders a bit – and what about the poor polar bear –? And stop, lest we forget Herbert the humble hedgehog. [*Beat*] Plants before plastic. That's what I say. That's who I am. The letter I found in my office on my desk, right on top of a pristine architectural drawing all smelly, inky and on funny paper.

Fay: Yes … how clever of you, Mr Bricks.

Billy: Turnips. [*Moodily*] Or rather rodents, from a rodent branch of the big turnip tree. [*Beat*] It was a back-street book shop at Camberwell Green. I came upon a book called *The Art of Memory*.[1] And I thought it might come in handy for business transactions ... [*a conspiratorial tone*] things to be kept quiet inside the head.

Fay: Yes. To remember. I did the same once, myself. I made up a –

Billy: Things not quiet kosher. I've got so much to show – you'll see. It's fantastic here! This place is just brimming with art and antiques. And we'll take Father, Freddie and the dog for a picnic in our bluebell wood. And I would like you to note, that I personally organize a grey squirrel hunt, with the boys, every now and again, to allow the little ginger fellas a chance to step up. [*Beat*] Courtesy of Mr Darwin. [*Deadpan*] I've even heard applause from the lawn. [*Beat*] And that every now and again, or at least once a week, a couple of the little bastards end up in the pot ... kinda symbolic. Not tonight though. No. Roast beef and Yorkshire pudding tonight. And I would also like you to know, that just sometimes I go for a long and lonely ... and stop and stand quiet still. And just listen to the birds and bees ... and then wait and just watch till the stars come out real slow ... and then hold my breath for a bit, and listen to the earth breathe ... in and out, like. [*Beat*] Yeah. We can't keep fiddling and fibbing about the planet. [*Beat*] Can we? [*2 beats*] Fay?

Fay: Yes?

Billy: I'm nature's friend here.

Fay: Yes, yes. Good for you. But where exactly are we?

---

[1] See reference list at end

Billy: I told you. You're outside Tunbridge Wells. Care for a slice of apple pie?

Fay: No.

Billy: It's nice. They're home grown.

Fay: No.

[*Beat*]

Billy: How about a nice peach, then?

Fay: [*Curt*] No.

Billy: Sure?

[*Beat*]

Fay: I'll wait for my brother.

Billy: Hurry up Freddie boy!

Fay: [*As if suddenly remembering*] I do believe I have seen you before. [*2 beats*] You're the mysterious Mr Money Bags. And you bid for the Chartridge Emeralds, at Daddy's auction a few years ago.

Billy: [*Aggressively*] I got'em! 2.5 million!

Fay: Mmn. Yes. Good for you. But we have met before?

Billy: No. Not really. [*Beat*] No.

[*Pause*]

Fay: Didn't I see you at Sony Eckart's photographic exhibition at The Hamilton?

Billy: I saw you.

[*2 beats*]

Fay: We were not introduced?

Billy: No. Not really. But I saw you.

[*Pause*]

Fay: Were we ever introduced?

Billy: Not that I remember. No.

[*2 beats*]

Fay: I know. I remember! It was at the auction. You had trouble with a cufflink ... you were fiddling with it and it dropped to floor. And you had to crawl about helplessly amongst the Prada and Chanel, poor chap ...

Billy: Er – well ... yeah. I got it here.

Fay: The cufflink?

Billy: Yes – er, no. Er – I mean – yes. I have them here.

Fay: Your cufflinks?

Billy: Here! Here in the castle! In a safe in a velvet box ... the emeralds!

Fay: Oh. The jewels. Yes. Good for you. A great charity. A worthy cause.

Billy: [*Mumbling*] 2.5 million.

Fay: Yes. Daddy actually pointed you out –

Billy: W-What did, did Daddy say? Why did Daddy point me out?

Fay: Well ... after all, you were a key player.

Billy: What did Daddy say?

Fay: I believe Daddy told me you were in the property business. Do you actually know, Daddy?

Billy: In passing ... yeah.

Fay: Well. Unfortunately, Daddy got himself involved in some rather bad business ventures, and it has affected his health for quite some time now – but of course you would know.

Billy: Yeah – yes. I had heard about it ... yes.

Fay: We aren't well off anymore, you know. What with medical bills, and all that. In fact, we're just about holding on to the town house, while Daddy continues to exist in some grandiose dream. And Freddie, well, Freddie's so indiscreet. I imagine you are aware of his little habit?

Billy: But that's why you're here! That's the birthday surprise. I'm a great fixer. I'll look after Daddy – no problem. And I'll sort out the dear boy's little hobby, too.

Fay: Really!

Billy: Of course.

[*Pause*]

Fay: This is quite impossible ...

Billy: I'm simply Freddie's friend. Has he never ever referred about me to you?

Fay: Mr Bricks. I am not au fait with my brother's present society.

[*2 beats*]

Billy: You just say the word, Fay!

Fay: I really must speak to my brother. This is all quite overwhelming ...

Billy: By all means. Do talk to the dear boy. And take lots of long lazy walks, together. Relax*avous*! I actually own bits and pieces of The Crescent, you know.

Fay: My Crescent!

Billy: Er-well – yeah. I do own a few little things in quite a few little places. Like terraces and squares and such. Funny. But as a kid as long as I had a few jiggles in me pocket for the pictures, fish 'n' chips, and the regular Saturday night gherkin, I was as happy as a sand boy.

But then Ma, Ma made me realize that you have to do the best for yourself in life. Although I do sometimes wonder if it's all worth it. The nods, the whispers, the secret handshakes – and what for? I ask you what for? I'll tell you what for ... the mere accumulation of coinage, the abject adoration of the Golden Calf, the inner sanctum of the silver dollar – that's what's for!

Fay: [*Studies* **Billy**] According to Francisco López de Gómara, 'when the Aztects of Mexico had familiarized themselves with the mores, the cultural habits of the Spanish Conquistadors, they became rather puzzled by the Spaniards' extraordinary interest in a certain yellow metal. In fact, they never seemed to stop talking about it. The natives were not unfamiliar with gold – it was pretty and easy to work, so they used it to make jewellery and statues, and occasionally used gold dust as a medium of exchange. But when an Aztec wanted to buy something, he generally paid in cocoa beans or bolts of cloth. So, this Spanish obsession with gold seemed quite inexplicable to them. And what was so important about a metal that could not be eaten, drunk or woven and was too soft to use for tools, or weapons of war? When the natives questioned the great *reptilian* Hernán Cortés as to why the Spaniards had such a passion for gold, the Conquistador replied ... "Because I and my companions suffer from a disease of the heart which can be cured only with gold ..."'[2]

[*Silence*]

Billy: Well, well – there you are, there you are ... thank you, Fay. But, But I, I, I'd all of a sudden think to myself how warm and comfy a cashmere overcoat, and how nice and soft a pair of crocodile shoes – and well,

---

[2] See references at end

unfortunately that just about settles it. [*Beat*] Still we all have our own little mores and cultural habits, don't we Fay? [*Pause. Upbeat*] And I do have plans. Real big plans ... visions, in fact.

Fay: Not for The Crescent, surely?

Billy: Now don't you going worrying yourself over your nice little Crescent. [*Flippantly*] I'm here and I'm there and I'm round and about.[3] Seriously though being a property developer is rather like being a magician: an illusionist, in fact. We chaps, we deal with intangible possibilities, like what is beyond the reasonably acceptable in social terms of course. I know we're quite often reviled, but we're also important chappies, too. Now take the word regeneration. Now, that's a nice little eco-friendly word that the politicians like to use, and the public like to hear. I can always find something to knock down, even in the most sedate of areas, with the help of a couple of bowler hats off the local golf course. There's always a wafer-thin piece of corner to build a nice big pay packet on. And the odd fire, or riot, and well – a presto! Regeneration. In fact, we're regular heroes for about five minutes. Also, a couple of trees and a pot of paint in some shit hole suddenly becomes Berkeley Square, along with big brownie points, and, just perhaps, a trip to Buck House. It's not nice, and it's not pleasant behaviour, but like Ma said: you have to do your best in life. Just like that much maligned Sir Phil Green, and the Carillion boys, too –

Fay: Can you actually hear yourself! Obviously, your ethics reside at the local golf club.

Billy: What? Listen! Me and Phil we come from the same place. There's no free ride in life for the likes of us. I

---

3 See references at end

can't afford to be happy and idle like Winnie the Pooh. And I can't be doing good deeds for everybody else's favourite nephew all the time, day and night, as well. And I'd rent out a piece of sky if I could and make no apology for it! Because, because time tends to gallop its hoofs over people like me and Phil, if we're not careful – no silver spoon here! And I won't crawl my way to the grave, as a poor pensioner without portfolio, either! [*2 beats*] Listen. Like Phil, I'm just a passionate jovial businessman. [*Abrupt*] I'm actually thinking of writing a memory for The Dulwich Diverter!

Fay: [*Icily*] It's memoir – actually.

[*2 beats*]

Billy: Well, if it helps some poor sod, along the way, that's just fine! [*Silence. A conciliatory tone*] Listen. My business is also about patience, and vision too. A game of illusion, remember? The acquisition of land is about secret possibilities. Good and bad. It's about what's beyond the reasonable and expected. It's about good judgement. It's about twists and turns and perfect timing too. It's about keeping the fat lady up in air and giggling, [*Fore finger up*] and balanced on ya' finger. Illusion and reality, remember? [*Beat*] Now don't you go worrying yourself about your precious little Crescent ... [*Musing*] strange, it's a long way away from Ma's funny little shaking house, that's –

Fay: You live at The Ritz?

Billy: Not particularly. No. I told you. I'm nomadic. [*Cannily*] I'm here and there and I'm round and about. And I also like to stand on a street corner, too. And ponder a pretty little property, now and again. I'm thinking about one right now. Right at this minute. [**Fay** *is visibly uncomfortable*] And to mentally arrange people and places into a perfect setting. It gives me pleasure. [*Beat. Darkly*] And it sometimes helps. [*Pause*] I'd stand by my big window looking out over the Park with its bunches of trees here and there, and feel really sad at all that empty space. And then one morning as I stood there rather sad and philosophical, it just came to me in a flash. [*Beat*] Leb-en-strum. [*Silence*] LEB – EN – STRUM! [*Beat*] Living space!

[*2 beats*]

Fay: I'm not deaf. Lebenstrum. Yes. I do know what it means. But what exactly do you mean?

Billy: [*Covertly*] Cemeteries are the next big thing.

[*Beat*]

Fay: That's preposterous! You can't go digging up a cemetery as you would a building site. And you can't ignore religious practice either, which actually amounts to the same thing.

Billy: I'm not about to go digging anybody up! Or about upsetting anybody's religious practice. You don't think I don't think about my Ma down there when the moon and the stars are sitting up there in the sky, and me lonesome shadow is leaning right over Ma's grave? Well? [*Beat*] Listen. It just came to me in a flash. I'd been watching a documentary on The North American Indian. And in particular The Sioux. Apparently, trees are quite rare on the prairie, along with a few shrubs here and there, and of course the mighty cactus. So, when the Chief, or one of the elders die, they wrap the body up in a buffalo skin, and bundle it right up in the air, on what to my trained eye appears to be a highly dubious structure, indeed. I suppose to get as close as possible to the local sky god. And of course, up and away from the odd hungry coyote. And it got me thinking about the cemetery as an urban smoking gun. So, I started to ponder these new super materials, such as Graphene, like what the boffins are all talking about. And so, I put my head together with my architect, and we came up with the idea of a jointless structure that goes [*Makes a bubble shape in the air*] up like a bubble, with the internal design of a beehive, and so little or no disturbance at ground level. Of course, we will have to wait until the hi-tech can catch up with us. But when it does we'll be ready to go.

Fay: You wish to build a structure over a graveyard.

Billy: Cemetery! Cemetery. No. Not build. Inflate.

[*Beat*]

Fay: You wish to inflate some kind of plastic material over a cemetery.

Billy: Well. Yes. A super bubble, easy, clear and clean. No problem.

Fay: Yes. But whatever the hi-tech, you would still have the problem of the highly emotive nature of this business.

Billy: Well – yes, of course at first. But these new materials what's coming will alter the way people think, and do. Flats, shops and offices, and people living, working and playing in harmony right above the Mothers and Fathers. It's a religious ideal. The Jew, the Christian, the Muslim all living and going about their particular business right above the sleeping ancestor. [*A high moral tone*] No more the poor woeful widow trudging over muddy ground to stand in a biting October wind with a bunch of flowers for hubby. And what widow wants to wait till the weather dries up? And does a woman really want to stand alone under a forlorn and threatening sky? And remember this: there's all sorts of dodgy people wander about a cemetery. In fact, someone actually nicked a lovely bowl of daffodils I left for my Ma. Right! It was a nice splash of colour, considering the early arrangement. [*Abruptly*] Nope, Ma won't be waiting for me 'round the Christmas table', anymore – with – 'a go on then – go on, eat ya' plate up, boy' – yeah, and I don't reckon nature gives out any return tickets, either! Yep – in as a squirt, and out as a handful of dust, there's ya rub. She was always loyal to lavender … [*Musing*] always smelt of lavender, my Ma. Me watch, it just stopped. Me penguins twitched. And a little red robin pecked at the window pane. [*Beat*] Of course, we gave her a hearty Celtic farewell. [*2 beats*] Yeah, Ma, she suffered from the great forgetfulness. [*Beat*] And yes. Jews and Muslims and everybody else living and working and playing together in a kind of earthly paradise, right over their slumbering grannies. 'It would be both psychologically and physiologically peace on earth.' Or so my architect reckons. Plus! Free funerals for all funded by my sparkling commercial quarter. And that includes all those, like the Hindus, who wish to go up the chimney, too! Now that's what I call handsome. Now that's what I call good business.

Fay: You seriously wish to build a commercial complex on sacred ground –?

Billy: Over! Over. Well, yes.

Fay: Nonsense! And what about the physiological and psychological distress of such a venture? Let alone the social disturbance such a plan would incur?

Billy: Distress? It's all been sorted, believe me, Fay. It's all been worked out. Although my architect chappie and me – well, we did have a few emotional ups and downs about its actual finished shape. I fancied a doughnut. But he argued briskly for a bridge. So, to keep him happy we settled on the shape of a bridge. [**Billy** *shapes the air*] Like a Pan's Pipe. So, then I said what about a name that suggests a healthy athletic lifestyle – to lift the spirits a bit ... considering the situation, that is. Like, like a nice splash of colour, like The Air Bridge. But then he suggested the public might think the project was sponsored by Nike – well, I wasn't having that! [*Beat*] So, then I said, what about the Bridge of Sighs, as a kind of symbolic tribute ... in consideration. And he said in consideration of the symbolic history of the original – in Venice, Italy. Well, the public might look on with a rather jaundiced eye, like it was offensive, or in bad taste. Anyway, we finally settled on the Crystal Bridge, because it had a kind of Wizard of Oz quality about it. Yeah, he's a regular Wizard of Woz, himself. Yep, always all puffed up with what he calls 'the knives and forks of reality'. Social disturbance? No problem. We may have to cut down a few trees, but they'll be replaced by nice flowery shrubs. No problem. Disturbance? It's all been worked out at 0.01 per cent.

[*2 beats*]

Fay: But that's the mere fluttering of a leaf!

Billy: Let's not quibble over a decimal point, Fay. The maths speak for themselves. [*Beat*] We're talking quantum leap here. We're talking about a fluid based structure that will stay up for at least a 1000 years. We're talking realistic sense about 'macro population biology, and epidemiology.' Or so my architect says. Big boys' stuff. Anyway, any awkward graves we'd quietly transfer and sort out adequate compensation later on. Fay, we're talking about self-funding cemeteries, here. Business and Burial in Commerce. BBC – and no licence fee to pay for the privilege, either! I call that handsome. I call that good business.

Fay: I'm astonished at your plan, Mr Bricks!

Billy: Of course! Of course, in life, and in business, and I reckon in art, too, there's something I call the Percentage Room. And it's occupied by up to 99.9 per cent of stupid, unimaginative bastards. True? [**Fay** *concedes the point*] It's sensible. It's logical. [*Beat*] It's *Lebenstrum*. I mean Rome and Athens would never have got going but for people like me. Think of little Billy the Builder going about his business trying to talk up The Coliseum to the local Caesar. [*Beat*] And yet people like me are publicly reviled, and branded big bad boys. [*A look of total bewilderment*] And what exactly is the alternative, you may ask? Well, short of shifting you, me and everybody else into the likes of Epping Forest, and that would upset the Little Green Ninjas. Imagine, Ricky Rodent and Willy the Weasel, tied up at the top of a tree, and yelling their balls off … funny funereal games, right Fay? It's a real smoking gun. Anyway, just as soon as the hi-tech becomes available I'll put in a bid with the plans all nice and neat and ready to go. [*Impishly*] I've already got my little eye on Highgate, actually.

Fay: My Mother's buried there!

Billy: No problem. No worries. Progress – phew!

[*Humorously*] Me, I'm from The Golden Age of the Bricklayer, myself. And what with 3D building, and what my architect fellow calls Hyperform, well, it's all getting a bit like Origami. [*Musing*] Origami. Now that's a nice big round word. It kinda bubbles up outa the lungs, and sorta tumbles around the tonsils, and kinda rolls around the mouth, and then it sorta bounces softly, but sharply off the tongue, and then kinda somersaults noisily right over the gums ... Origami. Anyway, after that my architect, he gets a bit sci-fi, and over emotional about massive structures in space, like flying city states, like orbiting moons – progress. Phew! [*Wistfully*] Now that's what I call real estate. Now that's what I call good intelligent business. [*Beat*] Now that's what I call immortality. And my architect, he says, seconds away, in future time, about a 1000 things can happen. [*Impulsive and playful*] And listen to this: he said, he reckons, that if he ever falls asleep and wakes up to find he can't wipe his own arse, he'd Ping-Pong off the inner planets, slide down Satan, and make an abrupt U-turn around Pluto, and go straight up Uranus, on his way to the stars! [*A stony silence.* **Billy** *gives a brief laugh. Pause. He mumbles*] My architect, he said, he reckons ... [*Flustered*] er – well, he, he goes on in his whacky, wordy, way: Temples of Deception: Holy rock 'n' roll outa that well oiled universal myth making machine, is as absurd as inviting the Mad Hatter to apply Cartesian Coordinates to the problem of juggling 58½ flaky snowballs, filled with 58 ½ curly kittens each singing in chorus, a Christmas Carol, in pure Mandarin – in three-dimensial space – time! And thus condemning our particular form of planetary life to the roll of cosmic clown, on the starry stage of the universe – in my *O*'pinion! [*2 beats*] a bit puffy, right? He talks like a talking parrot suffering the shits – excuse me! [*Defensively*] at any rate we'll probably all have to wait until religion's all dried up, fed up, and pulled on its hiking boots, and wandered off to fuck up some other poor bloody planet ... 'fear and want',[4] he reckons. [*Upbeat*] But to speak on more sentimental matters, my architect and I observed a young woman stretched out, and sunbathing in an itsy, bitsy bikini, alongside her dead hubby's grave. And we wondered if it had happened on the honeymoon ... funny and sad, right, Fay? [*Abruptly*] We have met before.

Fay: Have we?

Billy: Not social. No. Not some charity do. No.

Fay: Where? When?

[*2 beats*]

Billy: I've watched you in your studio.

Fay: ... In my studio?

Billy: Yes.

[*2 beats*]

Fay: In my studio?

Billy: And outside your local, too.

Fay: [*Abruptly*] In my home?

Billy: Yes. And outside the Nag's Head, too – with the dog. And walking the dog in the park ... it's when you brushed past me and smiled at me –

Fay: In my home!

Billy: Only in your studio! Your studio! Yes. Remember I own bits and pieces of The Crescent ... [*abrupt and pleasant*] and remember this, every window belongs to an eyeball.

---

4 See references at end

[*Pause*]

Fay: Is this a sexual thing? [*A helpless denial*] Is it my house –? You want my home! My home!

Billy: Er – no. No! Relax*avous*! I'm, I'm … I greatly admire your work. And I've been quietly collecting your pots for ages. Here in a room in the castle, I have an important collection of your pots, plus! the big tapestry: 'The Last Cake Shop in Chernobyl', along with its radioactive wedding cake in the front window … nice touch. And well, at least, I thought it highly imaginative, and, really rather *avant-garde*. I admire your art!

Fay: You're a collector … You! [*Beat*] You're a collector.

Billy: Yes. I adore the colours and patterns on your pots. And I go quietly to all your exhibitions, when Freddie tells me you won't be there.

Fay: For heaven's sake! Why haven't you ever approached me?

Billy: Because, because … I thought you might find me rather uncouth, and not arty enough for you and your friends.

Fay: Rubbish! And you have a good collection of my work?

Billy: Yes. Here in a room in the castle, dedicated to your pots and pieces.

Fay: How flattering! Thank you. You've certainly helped pay some very steep medical bills.

Billy: [*Solemnly*] The pleasure is all mine. It's got real meaning for me. [*Abrupt and focused*] 'It expresses a pure meditation on the secret structure of nature, pertaining to the true philosophic uncertainty at the heart of the human condition'.

Fay: My Goodness! You've just quoted my agent.

Billy: Yes, yes! It's, it's a real panacea for me … but, but I don't really understand the shapes and symbols … not really. I love it but I don't really understand it.

Fay: [*Studies* **Billy**. *Abrupt and precious*] Well. From the beginning of my creative life, my life, my work, my art, has been a pursuit, a meditation on the structure of nature. A private dialogue in plastic terms between the observer and the object: a bird, a leaf, a tree. A highly stylized search for a vision, an alphabet, a visual language of form and symbol. An approach to understand the underlying principle, and sublime elegance of nature's geometry. In fact, my very own little adventure begins 3000 years ago, and half a world away in China, in –

Billy: No! Not China Pots – your pots!

Fay: [*Drily*] And I thought you might have enjoyed my little *potted* history, Mr Bricks?

Billy: Billy, please.

Fay: Well. I'm going to surprise you, Mr Bricks. Consider a precocious school girl, whose, only real wish was to endear herself to her rather brilliant, if troubled Mother. And, so, rather like yourself, I memorized particular dynasties, styles and sites in ancient China. And introduced them into some amusing, if rather silly, freewheeling little verses [**Billy** *goes to speak*] – here goes:

> There was a young man of Ming,
> who worked in a kiln at Wa-Ch'a Ping.
> And who decided he really
> Did need a fling.
> But, oh dear! He did such a silly thing.
> And awoke the next morn to the dreadful dawn

Of discovering a purple
Ting on his Ding.
He roared an oath both wild and sore:
'Hunon! Honan!' And 'Hop-Hopei!'
In real smooth bluish Ch'ing.
And yes! Even as the purple Ting
transformed itself into
A yellow Mei-Ping.
And all because of a Shang Tang thank ye mam – yes!
Into a yellow Mei-Ping.
He gave a mighty sigh: 'Shu-Fu!'
And awaited the last of
A porcelain moon in a midnight sky
to say … bye-bye.
So sad his last sweet Song,
Sung to the tune of a rare Black Swan,
to sooth and rest his yellow Mei-Ping,
in the family tomb at Ying Ch'ing.
Just due south by west of old Peking.
Oh dear, what a terrible thing –
Howzat!

[*Reflectively*] And yes, I do believe I detected the briefest, fleeting ghost of a smile … yes. I don't know about you Mr Bricks, but the busy behaviour of Ming Dynasty porcelain, along with an earlier disastrous introduction into the fussy, noisy behaviour of late Baroque and Rococo styles, has always made me feel rather crowded and claustrophobic … [**Billy** *looks sheepishly about the room*] as if the very air were completely sucked out of my lungs … Mr Bricks. In fact, on my very first visit to the V&A, with my Father – you must surely be aware as to the full extent of my Father's former philanthropic activities … [*Darkly*] Mr Bricks? [**Billy** *slowly, thoughtfully agrees*] Of course you are. Well, it became a fundamental awakening experience for me. Especially after the noisy, bellicose nature of some early Tang pieces. I, I suddenly found myself transfixed by the simple purity of Sung period porcelain. Self-colour, and undecorated shape filled my child's eyes ... with wonder, Mr Bricks. And in particular a small blue vase with a clare de lune glaze ... it, it seemed to fill its space with its own cold, clear moonlight. It was a truly rapturous moment. And I do believe my little child's heart vanished into that simple blue vase. And since you appear to be such an enthusiastic advocate of my work, it quite naturally brings me to some rather exciting news. I've recently moved away from the wheel – yes. And all because of a happy coincidence. I was asked to host a small intimate dinner party in order to celebrate Lord Effington's election to the board of the Hermaphroditus Gallery. Well, after dinner over brandy and cigars, Lord Effington happened to wander over to my fireplace attracted by some knick-knacks, I'd made for my very own pleasure. And in a typically Johnsonion mood, declared there and then that my little pieces would be cast up to 6 or 7 feet in time for the gallery's summer exhibition – absolutely unbelievable! And what's more, one particular piece is to be placed in the grounds of his country house, at Goring, under my personal direction ... a mere potter, Mr Bricks, can you imagine –

Billy: Excuse me. Pardon me. But may I intrude ...? [**Fay** concedes] Those little knick-knacks. Those little studies above the fireplace ... would there be a common theme amongst them?

Fay: Yes. Yes, there would?

Billy: A natural common theme?

Fay: Why, yes?

Billy: Ah! … A natural common theme. And would that natural common theme be to do with a natural common shape, in a natural way?

[*2 beats*]

Fay: Yes …?

Billy: And would that natural common shape of those natural common objects, be found in an aquatic environment –?

Fay: Why – yes, Yes, they would …?

Billy: Mmnn. Fish!

Fay: [*Smugly*] No, no Mr Bricks … no.

Billy: Mmmnn. Jellyfish! [*Pause*] Jellyfish?

[*2 beats*]

Fay: A 7-foot bronze jellyfish – really … Mr Bricks?

Billy: [*Watches* **Fay**] And would the original shape of this favourite object in particular earmarked for Effington's garden, sit upright and taper to a point?

Fay: [*Taken aback*] Why, yes it would.

Billy: And would that particular piece, that original particular piece in particular have an original height of … say, 11.50 centimetres? [*Silence*] And would that particular piece in particular have an original diameter of say … 12.35 centimetres …?

Fay: [*Quietly*] Unbelievable ….!

Billy: And would that original piece, that original piece in particular be found in a museum in –

Fay: Entemnotrochus –

Billy: [*Triumphantly*] Adansoniana! [*Toneless*] A seashell.

[*Silence*]

Fay: You're very well informed, Mr Bricks.

Billy: [*With sarcasm*] Billy, please.

Fay: How on earth!

Billy: Now. That nice particular piece. That favourite particular piece. The 7-foot seashell for Effington … well. It's actually sitting right now downstairs in my garden. At this very minute. In my garden.

Fay: [*Abruptly*] But, but Lord Effington?

Billy: I personally purchased it off Effington … in person. Me, myself, I.

[*2 beats*]

Fay: He wouldn't?

Billy: He would. And he did.

Fay: But – he … how? Why …?

Billy: Let's just say I shivered his timbers, with a few ancient yarns. Yeah. He was just like a little pygmy mouse, drinking water at a waterhole, with his eyes keeping an eye on his arse.

[*Pause*]

Fay: You're very clever, Mr Bricks.

Billy: [*Playfully*] Billy, Billy! I thought I'd keep to the water theme. So, I put it up down there beside the lake. Near where Mike and Mable settle down for the night. I'll show you in the morning. I'm quite sure you will appreciate the setting. And Mike and Mable they just love it. And it's lovely just to watch their big happy gormless faces, just happily scratching away up and down all Ambrosian and blissful, like. In fact, it's quite pastoral.

Fay: [*Annoyed*] Anyway I've been seriously rediscovering myself: my life, my art, my vision in the light of my acceptance into a higher form of expression, Mr Bricks. [*Beat*] The eye to inform the mind, of beauty or bewilderment ... I'm, I'm actually daring to consider myself in the same creative gene pool as Vantorgerloo, and, and in consideration of my future work in terms of mathematical formulae. [*Solemnly*] I have become a disciple of De Stijl aesthetic, and the theoretical morphology of the biologist D'Arcy Wentworth Thompson. But I'm afraid at present all that exists are a few pencil drawings. [*Pompously*] I worship the cone, the cylinder and the sphere – *Mr Bricks*.

Billy: [*Beat*] What! What! More seashells –?

Fay: I beg your pardon!

Billy: [*Nervously*] Well – well, I shall certainly put my name down for the other bronzes – right away.

Fay: Really!

Billy: [*A fatherly tone*] Of course my dear. And further more I cannot count the seconds enough towards the revelation of your future work. And I shall be buying up all your mathematical formulae, too.

Fay: [*Cynically*] You'd really buy my work unseen?

Billy: Of course, my dear! It has to do with our family motto: Learn or Burn.

Fay: ... [*Puzzled*] Learn or Burn?

Billy: That's right. You have it, and you deserve it. And what you really need right now is some quiet thinking place, free from all the domestic ups and downs that so vex the sensitive artist. A truly tranquil place in order to make your very own particular kind of magic … yes, away from all the trials and tribulations that so beset the average person – and yes, with staff to support you 24/7. And may I beg your pardon my dear, but I have suggested to Freddie you come and stay at the castle.

Fay: But –

Billy: For as long or as short as you –

Fay: Yes, but –

Billy: And come and go as you please, of course.

Fay: That's very generous of you, Mr Bricks. But Lord Effington has invited me to stay at his country house for the summer, and I've already accepted.

Billy: Tut-tut. Effington's a funny fella, and has even funnier tastes, too. I do beg your pardon, my dear, but, but what you need right now is a sense of balance in your life.

[*Beat*]

Fay: A sense of what!

Billy: Er-yes. Er. A place of peace and quiet – and contemplation. And Effington runs a very busy household, indeed.

Fay: Oh good! I love busy.

[*Pause*]

Billy: I hope you don't mind, my dear. But you really do need to slow your life down a bit – I refer to the artist inside you.

Fay: [*Studies* **Billy**] And in what way do you suggest I slow my life down *a bit*, Mr Bricks?

[*2 beats*]

Billy: Well. I do hope you don't mind my dear. But all this coming and going and social stuff with this and that one ... well.

Fay: And who exactly is this and that one – Mr Bricks?

[*Pause*]

Billy: Well – er. Excuse me. But like that TV archaeologist fella on the telly.

[*Beat*]

Fay: Michael!

Billy: Yeah. The one on the telly. The one who talks like there's someone else's pet woodpecker pecking at his cords. The one I've heard can hear a rabbit fart in a field in Essex, whilst standing and whistling under Big Ben in Westminster. The one who always turns up at a dig all hygienic and immaculate, just after some poor bloody student has just dug up half a potato field in Cumbria, in December, to find a Viking jock strap!

Fay: How dare you!

Billy: [*Impulsively*] Yeah – Micky! The one with big ears, and a Micky Mouse nose! The one who always turns up after it's stopped snowing all hygienic, and with a spray tan – well, he's bad news, Fay. I've watched him in the toilet in the pub in The Nag's Head watching himself in the mirror. He's a very funny fella, that one. Very careful. In fact, what kind of a man pops in the pub for a pint, and just about everywhere he goes, and just about anywhere you fancy, and starts to disappear every 15 minutes, or, so, to find his own reflection – without even a medical condition to talk about? I reckon there's something funny going on there. I mean it's not natural for a chap just to stand

and stare at himself – to hunt down a mirror
everywhere he goes ... it's not normal, it's just not right,
it's just not done for a fellow to stand that still, in that
position, in that particular relationship, for that length
of time – yeah, bold upright, like there was a rod stuck
up his arse. And do you know what for? I ask you what
for? [Beat] I will tell you what for ... in short, in silent
tribute to this, this tiny flaxen quiff, that, that curled
itself up into a wispy kiss? That's what for! It's not
healthy. It's just not done. You could do much better for
yourself, Fay. A nice regular guy, with strong family ties
... not a man with a psychological reflective problem –
no – not, not someone, who, who, probably, happily,
joyfully, enjoys Holy Communion up close with a bottle
of cologne, sprayed with gratitude over a face that had
fallen in love with itself a long time ago. While all the
while sitting upright stiff, with his trousers 'round his
ankles, and with his bare, naked arse perched
precariously on the edge of the sacred golden crapper,
as he strained in a slow salute to nature, while all the
while his left hand rests regally on a perfumed roll of
lavender toilet paper. And all the while staring
hypnotically at, at a hapless, innocent mirror – most
probably! A man who every time he sees you – even in
the street, leaps across the road to sing a funny little
song, do a funny little dance, which ends up in a funny
little bow. [2 beats] I think he thinks he's a flower. [Beat]
And I reckon he should be dropped off at the nearest
garden centre – excuse me! And do remember: he may
have the cut of an aristocrat – but in reality, he's got the
pocket of a peasant. [Beat] But what you need is a man
who is able to take care of you, in the style your dear
Father was able too. A good plain-speaking man, with
nice family values ... and great expectations.

[*Silence*]

Fay: Mr Bricks. You have preyed upon me. You have preyed upon my family. And you have insulted a dear friend –

Billy: No! [*Silent frantic denial*]

Fay: You are a predator. You are a beast of prey –

Billy: No! I'm not!

[*2 beats*]

Fay: You have snooped into my financial affairs, and evidently manipulated yourself into my poor brother's –

Billy: I didn't! I haven't … relax*a*vous!

Fay: And yes. You have insulted a dear friend, and obviously threatened and intimidated an important associate – and, furthermore you have abducted and terrorized me, and no doubt traumatized my dog. And like a ghost invited yourself into my home. Mr Bricks, you eat up, you gobble up, you digest, and you defecate over all about you.

Billy: Please! No! No!

[**Billy** *drops to his knees, and crawls at her feet.*]

Please – please! You must understand – I, I admire you! I have been considerate and sensitive to your every need – and, and all I did was watch you from across the street … I worship and adore you. Abuse you? No! Never! Not I! [*Beat*] When the boys unrolled you at my feet –

Fay: I was brought here in a carpet?

Billy: Er – well … yes.

Fay: You actually had me rolled up and brought here in a bloody carpet –!

Billy: For your care and safety –

Fay: And held together no doubt by two pieces of string!

Billy: It's 12th Century Persian and very hygienic. And the expert, he says he reckons it has a love poem with secret kisses, woven into the weave.

Fay: [*Abruptly*] I don't care if it warmed the arse of Kublai Khan! You have violated me, my body, the temple of my soul –

Billy: [*Pleading*] Please! The boys were very careful – see! Not even a scratch, no! Not even a bruise – no! [*Beat*] Just perfect … not even – even … ev …

[*The beautiful voice*]:

The couch she lay on, like burnished gold,[5]
Burned golden with golden mermaids,
Dolphins and fishes, too.
As if just seconds before she had been stolen from a grotto in the sea.
A precious pearl brought up from the purple deep.
An alabaster Venus,
Blown gently on a scented breeze: a perfumèd gift,
Given by a mysterious sea,
Sighing, softly, softly … the sea, the sea … the sea…

[**Billy** *slumps back on his haunches.*]

[*Silence*]

Fay: [*Abruptly*] O! O! Your silly Shakespeare, rattle! Are you attempting to beguile me, Bricks? [*2 beats*] You really are a cunning little creature.

Billy: [*Confused. His normal voice*] You. You are not generous or gentle.

[**Billy** *looks up at her.*]

---

5 See references at end

I am not a creature. I do not live amongst the trees. Nor do I wallow in the mud, or eat my own shit. I am not rude, or uncivil.

[**Billy** *slowly stands up, and stares beyond her.*]

See! I stand upright. I am a man. [*Beat*] I know I am not elegant, or artistic ... or beautiful. And I know I've never been the target of unwelcome applause. But there are other qualities to being a man. Like, like constancy, and fortitude ... and purity of feeling. I'm like Ma's old lumpy armchair. Safe, cosy and dependable. [*Beat*] I know I frighten you, Fay. But I mean you no harm. Quite the opposite in fact. And I know you probably see me as over 3-quarters dead. And I reckon, you reckon I'm ready for a Roman bath ... I reckon. But, if you might just peep behind this mask, you might just encounter such possibilities, it might just take your breath away. [*Pause*] Do you think you might get used to me? [*Beat*] Take me. Accept me. Accept Billy Bricks, and I'll lay my little kingdom at your feet.

Fay: [*Slowly, pointedly, inspects him up and down*] You appear to be a creature vested in the fine art of patience, cunning and bafflement, Bricks. A creature of some basic instinctual intelligence: you watch, you listen, and you wait – yes, essentially sly, and *reptilian* by nature ...

Billy: [*Dangerously*] Then beware my snappers!

[Billy *returns to the chair and sits down brooding.*]

Your Ma wouldn't like you talking to me like that –

Fay: How dare you refer to my Mother!

Billy: Ah! The sacred cow ...

Blackout

2

A country road. A yellow moon.

Freddie *and* **Dido** *are seen motoring directly towards us at great speed.* **Freddie** *is intent, while* **Dido** *sniffs at the air. An owl is heard to hoot.* **Dido** *growls. The hoots recede. Silence. A horse is heard to neigh.* **Dido** *barks.* **Freddie** *a thunderous face. The neighs recede. Silence. A sheep is heard to baa.* **Dido** *growls.* **Freddie** *a thunderous face. The baas recede. Silence. A pig is heard to snort.* **Dido** *barks.* **Freddie** *a muttered oath. The snorts recede. A long silence. A duck is heard to quack.* **Dido** *barks –*

Freddie: Shush! Shush!

[*The quacks recede. A long silence. A cow is heard to moo.* **Freddie** *alert. The moos recede. A brief silence. A fox calls.* **Dido** *howls.* **Freddie** *curses loudly –*]

Blackout

3

The Room.

Billy, Fay.

Billy: [*Still brooding*] Yeah. I found her. I actually picked her up out of the gutter with her shoe trailing a roll of lav paper fluttering all prettily in the breeze – yes! I discovered her and fed her like a little nippled god. And it was over 27 years ago, that I first watched her slowly come up out of the public toilet on Tower Bridge Road, with her eyes all big and shiny and lit up all funny like. She tripped up a crack in the pavement and landed at my feet. [*Beat*] Like a pearl she was washed up against my boot. [*Abruptly*] Not toffee-nosed Belgravia – no. But big bad Bermondsey – that's right!

Slow Fade

4

The Wood. Moon shadow.

Freddie, Dido.

The car is parked. **Freddie** *and* **Dido** *are seen sitting in the car.* **Freddie** *peers nervously into the night, while* **Dido** *continues to sniff at the air. Silence. An owl is heard to screech.* **Freddie** *cowers.* **Dido** *growls.* **Freddie** *curses. Silence. A nightjar is heard to call.* **Dido** *alert. It calls.* **Freddie** *about to curse. Silence. A fox is heard to call.* **Dido** *howls.* **Freddie** *curses under his breathe. Brief silence. The owl is heard to screech.* **Freddie** *looks sharply up at* **Dido**. *Pause. He relaxes. A fox calls.* **Dido** *howls.* **Freddie** *curses –*

Blackout

5

The Room.

Billy, Fay.

Billy: — Yeah. It was there and then I picked her up and cleaned her up, and dabbed her lovely face with a big clean handkerchief from right out of my pocket. And it was there and then, right there and then, that she took me and showed me her art hanging from the church railings at St Mary's, in the market place. I actually funded your Ma, your Mother. I actually financed her early career in chalk and charcoal drawings from two burnt-out buildings, and a fruit and veg stall. I bought her pencils and paints and brushes, and watched her paint her dots and spirals and such. And I gave her a bed and pocket money, too. And then I stepped back and watched the flash gits arrive, the big boys and girls in fancy cars – the fairies, the flatterers – the intelligentsia! Along with your Honourables and the big society bashes, and weekends away – like forever. And in all that time I watched and waited and hoped for a kinda harmonious harmony to come back for a bit into our lives. I believed in your Ma, your Mother … I actually thought my little boat was fit to sail all the way to the moon. And I cleaned her up and bought her some nice clothes, and some real nice bling, and a nice little car, too. And I hoped and I believed and I put up with her comings and goings and quick-change routines in and out from my little flat in Snowfields, along with the little dog I bought her, as I always fondly remembered that day that she first came up and out of the public toilet in Tower Bridge Road all bright and bushy tailed … just like Venus she was.

[Silence]

Fay: *[Deeply puzzled]* There must be some confusion, Mr Bricks. My Mother was raised and spent most of her early working life in Windsor.

Billy: *[Impishly]* Ah! The mysterious Mummy.

Fay: *[Exasperated]* Is this about business? Does this whole charade have anything to do with Freddie? *[2 beats]* Well? Does it? Because Freddie is unwell. You must be aware of my brother's unfortunate life style. And Freddie's judgement is not to be trusted, Mr Bricks – if, I can only –

Billy: *[Playfully]* Windsor. Now that conjures up a nice pastoral picture, especially with a bunch of sheep strolling about. And of course, the dear little grandmamma all podgy and chuckling and sitting pretty in her big flowery armchair in her tiny gingerbread cottage all wisteria and sunny and lovely, and happily bouncing her two little darlings up and down on her fat chubby knees, amongst giggles, fizzy pop, and fruity cake, for Mum, Dad and the kids. Real home made with her very own dimpled fingers – yeah, and ripe with raspberries she'd picked from the nice garden, and all washed down with a nice big pot of tea. Ah! What a delightful picture –

Fay: *[Sharply]* My grandparents were doctors. And they died in an epidemic in the Gamba before we were born, Mr Bricks.

Billy: What! No chocolate box memory? No gingerbread cottage? Not even a captured souvenir? Nor even a faded brown photo ...? What! No fleetingly blurred farewell to dear Olde England? Well, well, well! it sounds a bit like the fable of the fella who caught a duck's fart in a butterfly net, to me.

Fay: [*Confused*] Windsor has never had any meaning for us …

Billy: Good! Because over 27 years ago, your Mummy, your Ma sprang up in bangles and beads from a Stone Age settlement round the corner from the Windsor Castle public house off the Edgware Road, where she fed the fantasies of the local wild life of West London, to feed her little hobby – yes! Especially with that cartoon on her right arm, going up and down like a water pump. It was like being back at the pictures with a Saturday night gherkin. [**Fay** *is visibly shaken*] I can't count the times I've smacked up a nice fat juicy vein on her regal backside, in the bog at the back of the pub – true. Me and her, and her, sitting side saddle on the lav and balanced like a trapeze artiste, and her squeezing hard and me flicking up a fix for her busy little bum – me. Me! Bubbly Billy Bricks. Mr *H*ygienic. [*Beat*] True. And then I goes and cleans her up and fills her up full of methadone and good fresh food, and quiet walks in the park, and sunbathing at the seaside, too. And then – hey presto! All of a sudden, like overnight her shit don't stink! And she becomes all grandiose and piss elegant, and suddenly the oracle according to Jackson fucking Pollock, on wriggles, squiggles and splodges. And then there's this whole parallel life come into existence, along with a fancy flat, and maid, and an endlessly rotating door all 360 degrees of Hims and Hers – and Them! Well, I didn't need the eyeballs of a skate to see what was going on. [*2 beats*] And yes, you can mend a broken nose, Fay. And I watched, and I waited, and I found myself slotted in for Thursday afternoons, with the pictures, a pint in the pub, and a bench amongst the pigeons in Trafalgar Square, with a brief stroll hand in hand down The Strand, and her all dressed down like in disguise. And me like, treading heavy the years and carrying in me pocket a bag full of empty promises, and waiting and watching, and her without a sorry in her spittle, and me waiting beside a tree, and watching up at her window, and that endlessly rotating door, autumn, winter, spring, I even got familiar with the planets, and easy with the local road sweep, and kinda friendly with the premadonna dancin' dustman and it goaded me up to achieve. And I did achieve, and with a few more insurance jobs, I got suitable suited and booted and living right up there in the street from her flat. [*Beat*] I had achieved. I had arrived ... but it wasn't enough. [*Beat*] It was me. [*Beat*] It was I. [*Beat*] I was not luminous. I did not shine. [*2 beats*] I did not glitter ... Many years ago, when I was a boy and Banjo was tiny, and I'd just started working a fruit and veg stall at London Bridge Station, there was a boy there who came to the attention of The British Athletic Association, probably from a bowler hat off a train, and on its way to do a dodgy deal in Threadneedle Street – perhaps? Because this particular boy was able to jump from a standing position in hobnail boots, and land safely on top of a red post box ... yeah. He didn't go for it though, because back in those days it was all legend and no lolly. In fact, my Ma used to say I could've been a professional cricketer, if we'd come from Surbiton ... And it was one bright and cheery morning over 28¾ years ago, I noted, I observed, I sensed a change in her body work, when she walked into her sitting room all dressed up and perfect, and attentive to the maid, and attentive to the room, like plumping a cushion here, and smoothing the fold of a curtain there. And whereas before she'd be slow and moody to wash and dress before late afternoon. Here she was playfully dancing and kissing the maid, and kissing and cuddling her little dog Snowflake. And as I said all attentive to every detail ... and to cap all that downstairs there's this ancient arty fella slowly rotating the door all 360 degrees with a bunch of flowers ... and – bingo! She finally goes and settles on some old fart with the sperm count of a Charlie Chaplin. Ring any bells? Do you feel informed? Have I painted a pretty enough picture ...? And the clever little minx marries up to that big lovely house in Highgate. Yeah, with 2 sproggs and a dog. D'ya kinda remember? The one with the yellow door, and wisteria all tumbling down like a purple waterfall. [*Thinking out loud*] And a few years along ... now, what did the local rag say ...? 'Prominent Mother attempts to hang herself in children's nursery.' [*2 beats*] Funny thing that. After all those years, she finally goes and gets it right at last. And actually, achieved big time art in the wine cellar at number 7 The Crescent, Belgravia, with a pair of David Hockney's braces, no less —

Fay: [*Whispered*] Mon chagrin ...

Billy: [*Lightly*] I beg your pardon?

[*Pause*]

Fay: [*Quiet and steely*] You preyed upon my Father. [*Beat*] You used my Mother's death. [*Beat*] You preyed upon my Father's grief. [*2 beats*] You are primitive and wild. [*Beat*] A savage in a dinner jacket. [*Beat*] A puffed up popinjay to the world, but in truth a devil! He realized too late your pernicious nature, your true hatred of moral and civilised behaviour, along with your dirty little deals, your victims and your crumbling Babel Towers ...! You, you are a pariah, a parasite, and a bringer of chaos to all about you!

Billy: What's that –? What's that? [*Cupping an ear*] Funny? But I thought I heard the echo of a cuckoo in a nearby cuckoo tree?

Fay: Your blackmailing! Your political backhanders! Your hoodlum family! Your climate of fear!

Billy: Tut-tut! Think of Athens, think of Rome, and consider little Billy the Builder.

Fay: [*Darkly*] You with your wide boy wallet, and dirty little games, oh yes, my Father learned all about you, you and your murky empire. He found out too late just who and what you where – are! As you crawled your way up into polite society, by buying up the bankrupt, the stupid and the greedy!

Billy: And what about you? You and her, and her, with her fancy airs and fancy friends, and fancy lip job all puffed up and like walking about looking like a fish – right! All safe and sound and floating about on your hoity-toity cloud, and feeding off your petty dislikes, and snooty hatreds, with your ponies and piano lessons – and her, her up there all easy and happy, and with, with, her hair all coloured up, like an artificial blonde, and swinging her legs in fur coat and no knickers!

Fay: My Mother was a good woman!

Billy: Coo-coo!

Fay: Mr Bricks. Or should I say Billy the Bailiff. You are a repugnant, bitter, brutish, overdressed, over coiffured clown, who has sniffed and dribbled his way over some of the finest tables in the country –

[**Billy** *jumps up.*]

Billy: I'm not a clown! I'm not a creature ...!

Fay: Coo-coo.

Slow Fade

6

The Wood.

Freddie, Dido.

Dark. Silent. A heron is heard to shriek. Startled birds are heard. They slowly settle. Silence. A nightjar is heard to call. Beat. It calls. Silence. A fox is heard to cry. 2 beats. It cries. Silence. Abrupt and close, the sound of bodies crashing through bush, along with the confusion of the startled wild life. Abrupt silence. The birds slowly settle. Sudden moonlight. Pause. **Dido***'s head pops out from behind a tree. The goggles are now hanging loose about her neck. She looks about with timid curiosity. 2 beats.* **Freddie***'s head appears resting on hers. He looks about nervously.* **Dido** *sniffs and begins to wander about.*

Freddie: [*Sharply whispered*] Get back here!

[**Dido** *stops. Sites down. Looks about, and then reluctantly returns to the tree. The owl is heard to screech. Both disappear behind the tree. Silence. The nightjar is heard to call. Beat. It calls. Silence.* **Dido***'s head pops out, and* **Freddie***'s follows.* **Both** *are watchful.*

Close: hunters with dogs are heard.]

Banjo: [*Booming*] Wi O' Kum!

[**Freddie** *and* **Dido** *disappear behind the tree.*]

Wi O'Kum!

[**Banjo***'s laughter is heard as the hunt moves on.*

Silence

Dido *wanders away from the tree, and settles down beside a bush.* **Freddie** *with great caution follows her, and sites down against the tree.* **Dido** *watches him, while grooming herself.*]

Freddie: Shhh! [**Dido** *yawns*] Shhhhhh!

[**Dido** *sulkily coils up, and continues to watch* **Freddie**.]

I wonder how did they know? [*To* **Dido**] Of course you simply couldn't resist making a spectacle of yourself in the car – I blame you! [**Dido** *whimpers. The owl screeches.* **Both** *alert. Silence. Both relax. To himself*] How close and in what direction?

[**Freddie** *stares long and moodily at* **Dido**. **Dido** *slowly stands up, and contemplates the scene.*

Quietly] I blame you ...

[**Dido** *walks over to him.*]

Dido: Now calm down. It's a hunter's moon. And we really do need a plan of action. We must out guess these people ... for Fay's sake. [*Pause*] Well get up! [**Freddie** *does not move*] Come on! Get up, and try to behave like a decent human being.

[**Freddie** *reluctantly stands up.*]

Everything you do is impromptu and chemically driven. Look at yourself. Your dress, your general behaviour ... and not a thought for the consequences of your actions – whatsoever!

Freddie: But, but Banjo's here – and so Billy must be here, too!

Dido: Obviously. But what about Fay ... Fay!

Freddie: [*Defiantly*] Yes! Exactly. That's why we need a plan. And that's why I've been so concerned!

Dido: [*Exasperated*] Well! Where is this fabled castle? And if we do happen upon it, do we need a ladder? Or is there a magic key under a magic flower pot?

Freddie: [*Temperamentally*] It's here! It's here! [*Looking about*] It's here, here ... somewhere ...?

Dido: [*Sneering*] Well, it might even have a marmalade moat, now wouldn't that reflect charmingly our marzipan moon –?

Freddie: [*Whispered*] Those two fiends are here! And the castle's here, too ...! [*Looking about. Accusingly*] I wanted to inform the police, remember?

Dido: With your recent history – I think not! Quite apart from the social ramifications of going public – think of Fay. And consider Father's good name, too.

Freddie: [*Spitefully*] Dad's away with the fairies! And I told you about this place – I warned you about it! It's full of fucking weirdos ... [*Anxiously looking about*] this place has been whispered about in town for ages ... it's a very peculiar place – believe me. And I warned you about Banjo and his bunch of thugs ... this is a crazy place ...

Dido: [*Impatiently*] Or have you simply invited me into one of your dreadful little nightmares? If so I will happily awake, refreshed on my favourite blanket, in my basket at number 7 The Crescent, W2? [*2 beats*] If not. If this is for real ... then, that vile little –

Freddie: Exactly! Exactly! [*Beat*] I wonder what shall we do, Dido?

Dido: Well, in the confusion I did happen to notice what appeared to be a path up ahead, unless of course it was a trick of the moonlight? Oh, and by the way – a little observation, you forgot to bring the torch.

Freddie: Oh – and by the way. You left the fucking headlights on.

[*2 beats*]

Dido: [*Calmly*] I did not.

[*Beat*]

Freddie: You did.

[*2 beats*]

Dido: I did not.

[*Beat*]

Freddie: Yes, you did!

[*2 beats*]

Dido: I did not!

Freddie: You bloody did!

[*2 beats*]

Yes, you bloody did!

[*Pause*]

Dido: [*Slowly, with definition*] I DID NOT –

Freddie: [*Aggressively*] You did! You –

[*The tiger roars. Brief tableau. They both scramble into a bush. The tiger roars. The bush trembles. The tiger roars.*]

Blackout

7

The Room.

Billy, Fay.

Billy: [*Sitting in the chair. Still angry*] Terry's getting hungry. And what about you! You and your arty farty so, so fragile sensibility ... and all that romantic tosh about a tiny pot with its six or seven itsy, bitsy pieces of moonlight floating about – and of course, that truly raptures moment when the dear little heart plopped into the dear little pot, as you stood their hand in hand with big bucks Daddy kins. And you and him got ready to toodle off back together into that rosy rainbow future, down a little lane populated by you and him, and couple dozen other foxy families able to slip the kids, the nephews, along with the odd bastard into any arty-crafty load of bollocks! So easy for Them and You and Him and Her! And all happy hanging about in fancy restaurants. And all pompous and posing like in cult galleries with a Him and a Her, and the likes of that funny little fella who goes about dressed up as Little Bo-Peep, or Betty Boo – or whoever!

Fay: How dare you!

Billy: [*Innocently*] I beg your pardon?

Fay: How dare you insult my family and friends! And if, if you are referring to the gentle soul who has laid bare his myriad identities on the high alter of public opinion in order in art to reveal a secret passion, or indeed, ordeal, Its origins, perhaps from some confused sibling hour, and by extension has challenged both public and critic alike into a serious understanding of contemporary ceramic art, other than merely a suburban twin-set, and pearl pastime? If! [**Billy** *begins to whistle Little Bo-Peep. Both progressively become louder*] If, if you are referring to the artist who has done rather more than any other in recent years to alter the public perception of the humble potter, and by token has risen phoenix-like, heroic and towering from the ashes of bias and discrimination? [**Fay** *lowers her voice*] Then yes! So, unlike the sly, spiteful creature [**Billy** *abruptly stops whistling, and watches her with malice*] who has crawled its way up, out of a sewer from some sub –

[*The tiger roars. 2 beats. The tiger roars.*]

Blackout

8

The Wood.

Freddie, **Dido**. The same.

Silence. The bush trembles in aggressive and punctuated whispers.

Dido: And you didn't think to tell me!

[*Pause*]

Freddie: It was because I didn't believe it myself.

Dido: Oh! It was just another silly rumour was it?

Freddie: [*Defensively*] I was actually thinking of Fay, Fay. And if you knew you might have changed your mind about coming here.

[*Pause*]

Dido: Well. What is it?

[*2 beats*]

Freddie: It's a cat –

Dido: Of course, it's a bloody cat! And according to a recent zoological paper, every bird, bat and bug in this damned wood already knows it's not a cuddly happy bunny hopping about amongst them. And since we appear to be in the vicinity of a gang of mindless hoodlums ... well, may I suggest we must also assume that it's not going to be a happy Mr Tiddles, that so happens to cross our path, either. So, in the interests of pure survival, I would dearly like to know just what precise specie of cat we might just bump into tonight?

[*Pause*]

Freddie: Well ... I think it's a tiger.

[*Silence*]

[*A great rustling of leaves, and Dido's head pops out from the bush. She carefully takes in the scene.*]

Dido: A night hunter – splendid! Well done Freddie! The perfect killing machine … it's just what we need! [*Thinking to herself*] No – not even, he … no.

Freddie: [*Apprehensive*] No? No? He …?

Dido: Of course, not … utterly ridiculous!

Freddie: What not?

[*2 beats*]

Dido: He simply wouldn't!

Freddie: Would not what?

Dido: No, not even … he …?

Freddie: He? He who would not what!

Dido: … He couldn't?

Freddie: [*Alarmed*] He who couldn't not what?

[*2 beats*]

Dido: Walkies …?

Freddie: Banjo!

Dido: [*To* **Freddie**] Certainly not!

[*Pause*]

Freddie: But, but, but … would he?

Dido: Not unless there is some other silly little rumour you haven't bothered to tell me about? Like a crocodile that patrols the flower beds? Or, perhaps a Gruffalo that is posing as the village policeman?

[*A great rustling of leaves, and* **Freddie**'s *head pops out from the bush to rest on* **Dido**'s *head.* **Both** *are watchful.*]

Freddie: That's all I know – it's, it's a tiger … and people have been invited down here ... and – well ...

Dido: [*Knowing*] And well what!

Freddie: And ... and of sort of –

Dido: [*With irony*] Afternoon *tea* with Mr Tiger ... perhaps? [*2 beats. Frostily*] Your penis is touching my bottom.

Freddie: [*Mortified*] Oh – oh!

[**Freddie**'s *head disappears to reappear next to* **Dido**'s *head.*]

I'm stressed! I'm stressed! [*Beat*] I do apologize, Dido.

[*Annoyed,* **Dido** *crawls out from the bush. And standing up begins to pick the leaves from her coat.* **Freddie** *follows her out, and stands watching her sheepishly. He goes to speak – she glares at him, and continues to groom herself.*]

Dido: [*Careful and reflective*] Do you remember how the house began to smell tropical, and Fay became feverish, and began to sleep walk again? And Rosie would look puzzled, and say. 'I cooks and I cleans, and it's all I do and it's all I knows.' [**Freddie** *agrees*] And how Fay continued to sleepwalk the stairs, the studio, the cellar ... like she did after Mother ...?

Freddie: [*A haunted tone*] Yes. Me too ... upstairs, downstairs, and objects moved and lost ... souvenirs, precious things, like Mother's emerald earrings, along with strange noises, and the movement of furniture ... like the tinkling of a chandelier – and remember what Rosie said. 'A spider could do that easy enough ...' do you remember? [**Dido** *agrees*] And the morning Fay was feverish again, and so I decided to take you for a walk in the park.

Dido: You remember!

Freddie: And we took our usual path into Kensington Gardens towards the pond. Yes. Where we picnic sometimes.

Dido: ... And it was a lovely blowy autumn morning with ripples right across the surface of the water.

Freddie: And the ducks and swans –

Dido: And the little sailing boats –

Freddie: All bobbing up and down!

Dido: ... And the children laughing and having great fun.

Freddie: – Remember the red and yellow kite?

Dido: – And how it appeared to wave at us high over the pond?

Freddie: Of course, I do.

Dido: [*Studies him*] And you spotted a gorgeous Vanessa Atalanta – remember? [**Freddie** *is confused*] And after that we came upon a fairy ring dotted with Agaricus Campestris ... do you remember? [**Freddie** *is still confused. Angry*] For goodness' sake, Freddie! A Red Admiral, and some common mushrooms!

Freddie: I, I ... don't remember ...

Dido: [*Gently*] It's what you were. It's what you are deep inside ... before. [*Cheerfully*] And the lovely yellow kite just hanging over the pond.

Freddie: Yes! Yes, I do.

Dido: The same yellow as my favourite rubber ball –

Freddie: Of course!

Dido: Which you threw into the air –

Freddie: I did, I did!

[*2 beats*]

Dido: [*Studies* **Freddie**] And off I went racing across the grass, until it bounced and it rolled and it came slowly to rest under the shadow of a blue shoe ... purple. And I looked slowly up at a long black fur coat, and up and over a gold Hawaiian shirt populated with sea-monsters swallowing hapless sailors, and up, and up until the monolith moved. And as it did the ground trembled, and the sun became as black as night ... and in the shadow my nose was touched by a cold silver skull with big emerald eyes ...

Freddie: [*Fearful*] Hypnotic.

Dido: [*Darkly*] Yes, yes. And the monolith laughed and it pinched my ear, and it blew deep into my nose ...

Freddie: Tropical?

Dido: [*Agrees. Beat*] Elemental.

[*2 beats.*]

Together: [*Whispered*] Banjo!

Freddie: [*Desperately*] It's all my fault – everything! It started out an easy-going weekend – easy and harmless. I dined alone in Chelsea at Bumpkins, and later went on to The Admiral Cod with Charlie, Josh and the Von Kleins, where we met up with Roland and the gang. And then together we all set off to do a little business at the Seven Dials – score a few lines – harmless really ... and yet, just about everywhere we went, like a shadow, like in Balthazar's – and even in every pissior along our way between harmless Buds and Bourbon shots ... there he was – him, hidden in laughter. [*A secretive, exoteric tonc*] 'Quis hunc nostrum chamaeleonta non foormido?'[6] [**Dido** *agrees*] And it was in there in the pissior in Balthazar that Roland overheard about a gig in a club in Hackney. So, later

---

[6] See references at end

we went slumming – and just so cool in amongst
those exotic creatures, so cool watching it watch itself
like some huge restless beast gazing in upon its own
infatuation … [*Abruptly*] it was all about chilling and
forgetting with Roland and the gang – [*Fearful*] then,
he – him, The Chameleon, he pinched my nose, and
blew deep into my mouth … [*Whispered*] 'dum
loquitur vernas efflat ab ore rosas.'[7]

Dido: [*Quietly*] Banjo.

[*2 beats*]

Freddie: Yes.

[*Beat*]

Dido: And Billy?

Freddie: Yes, yes. An oily little man in a rather garish suit, with
a yellow flower in the buttonhole.

Dido: [*Studies* **Freddie**. *Abruptly*] Glaucium Flavum.
[**Freddie** *is confused*] For goodness' sake, Freddie!
The Horned Poppy …!

Freddie: [*Still confused*] Yes, yes. A very peculiar little man –

Dido: I don't need a description of the little shit, thank you
very much –!

Freddie: I, I need – I would like Father if ever possible to
understand, and really know why I became so
confused by that little man. [**Freddie** *mimics* **Billy**
badly] 'Because I'd been so keen and patient and
looking forward to you knocking on our little door,
here. And after all I knows your Father, and respects
your Father because him and me are both
businessmen, too. And I do want to be a good
neighbour and friend to you both. And I have much
admired your family, and much admired your sister's

___
[7] See references at end

pots and stuff for a long time now, and your dear
Father's good deeds like forever, and of course I am
sorry to hear about your Mum, but do remember
even O'phelia – herself, had her ups and downs
because of a funny madness. And I know all about
you, you and your clever little head full of elephants,
zebras and giraffes. And your Father's recent illness –
and what about me mystery flowers I sent in honest
and humble hope they went down well with the sister
…' [*His normal voice*] and hello! You stupid bastard!
[**Freddie** *mimics* **Billy**] And I know all about the ups
and downs of the family fortune, at least, the whisper
goes so. And because I respect your Father so much,
and I've got a bread and butter approach, and a real
genius head for business, so, so, I say to you with the
greatest of respect – right now, sign here on the
dotted line, Freddie boy, and I'll resurrect the family
funds – and you get to keep the gold pen as a symbol
of the mutual trust and high regard between us – go
on Freddie!

[*2 beats*]

Dido: But you were given power of attorney …

Freddie: I know.

Dido: [*Exploding*] And you went and signed it over to him!

Freddie: I was bewitched – my silly butterfly spirit was
bewitched, and confused by that awful little man.
And we really did need financial help, remember?
[*Beat. He mimics* **Billy** *with venom*] 'No worries, bro!
Welcome to me magic parlour, come in, pull up a
chair, sit down and put your feet up on me table all
easy like, and dip your little nose into me sweetie
bowl, into me very own perspicacious cocktail, 'Cause
your every wish is my command – abracadabra!'

[**Freddie**'s *normal voice. Abstractedly*] My eyes flashed, my knees knocked, and the room flew madly about, and it seemed to me, that I tumbled down a rabbit hole, and into a twilit room … [*a hallucinatory tone*] that, that appeared to grow and grow into a twilight kingdom in a shifting landscape of whispers and laughter inhabited by a slow-moving emerald beast – before, before a sudden familiar fragrance, a sudden familiar voice that dissolved that spectral world into a thousand dear memories. [*Beat*] It, its sweetness came and went and was gone and drowned out by the thunderous roar of a waterfall, and moonlight and clouds of luminous insects dancing over gigantic water lilies, rising ghostly out of a feverish mist, below the screech and call of creatures in giant trees busy catching bats and moths, above a coiled snake silently suffocating a sleeping monkey, in the shadow of a big cat, watched by a black hawk-like hunter with green eyes – [**Freddie**'s *normal tone, breathless, dark*] it was then, then that I heard, felt, the hot earthy whisper of a lie – about us, us, and truly awful things about Mother … I, I must've blacked out, because I woke up in marshland, in water, to birdsong, with the sun rising over the Olympic Park… [*Softly*] and – yes. I heard Mother's voice – Mother's rabbit poem… do you remember?

[*2 beats.* **Dido** *nods*]:

> But I walked on the common,
> The old-gold common …
> And I saw little rabbits
> 'Most every – [8]

[**Banjo** *and the hunt are heard.*]

---

[8] See references at end

Banjo: [*Close and thunderous*] I've huffed and I've puffed and I've blown di winds, and scattered di clouds, and made naked di eye of di moon! And I'll leap di hills, and jump di churchy bell, in mi powerfil boots. I'll shake di trees, and tear up di roots, and throw'em deep in Di Devil Door! And wid mi nose I'll sniff up and down and roundabout every sneaky foxy hole! [*Teasingly*] It's big bad BoBo im come looking for thee – yowl! [*Imperiously*] I am di knife, I am di gun, I am di tunderous ting!

[*The hunt closer still.*

Freddie *and* **Dido** *crawl back into the bush. The tiger roars. The bush trembles. The hippos bellow. Brief silence. The bush trembles with heated whispers. The tiger roars. And* **Banjo**'s *laughter is heard as the hunt moves on. Silence. The bush trembles with heated whispers.*]

Blackout

9

The Room.

Billy, Fay.

Both *are listening intensely.*

Fay: [*Sharply*] Oh I know all about you. I was given a vivid description of your knockabout sense of fun, along with your high sense of style. And of course, your very own Planet, Pocket Credentials, when you happened to bumble your way into Mr PuzzlePotts' Gallery, dressed in a sable trimmed canary yellow overcoat, accompanied by a canary yellow suit, which was loudly applauded by a pair of yellow crocodile shoes. In fact, the whole ridiculous ensemble just perfect for the turnip-nosed buffoon in Dadaist art, and blowing green slime into an oversized handkerchief, until, that is, you decided to move majestically forth towards the high point of that whole dreadful misadventure, when you happened to sneeze, and knock over the key piece of my exhibition – *The Triumph of the Tomb over 10,000 Killer Bees*, of which, I might add were preserved and flown over at great expense from the Brazilian rain forest – whatever put you together Bricks, confused the clockwork!

Billy: [*Pleading*] It was the flu! The flu! I sniffed it all up, and out it all blew! It was an accident –! A pure, honest accident!

Fay: And you fled the scene –?

Billy: N-No! Not me, not I! I sent my driver back to pick up the pieces ...

Fay: [*Studies* **Billy**] Rather Humpty Dumpty wouldn't you say, Bricks? And that show piece was earmarked for Lord Effington, himself.

Billy: But I had the pot put together …

Fay: Yes, I did wonder what you had done with the pieces.

Billy: It's here in my collection, in the castle …

Fay: You mean hidden away in this lunatic asylum. In this zoo in the middle of nowhere.

[*She gestures to the room.*]

How wonderful! Such stars, and how beautiful the moonlight! And I suppose those rural noises I just heard was your brother settling down for the night with the hippopotamus –

[*A candle flickers and becomes still.*]

Billy: [*Softly, the beautiful voice*] Your art for me has always been the feel, the ghostly touch, yes, the proximity of your touch with its ghostly scent, against my warming cheek. And that particular piece, that particular creation, seemed to me full of 10,000 phantom kisses, like its 10,000 tiny solar bodies, cocooned inside honey and glass, and slowly revolving in its own silent grandeur. There, tiny invisible rays, warming each tiny beat, of my beating heart … yes, slowly revolving in those tiny, yellow tombs …

Fay: [*Abruptly*] Is that it? Is that your best shot? [*Beat*] So, the charade goes on, does it? Why don't you come out from behind that malignant bush you have been skulking behind for 28 and ¾ years – come on! [*2 beats*] Well. Is this it? The plan? A last chance assault on my sensibility, before a revaluation of the nature of this siege in all its utter futility – well? [*Pause*] Or, are we about to go back to good old rape and pillage? Because we both know the pillage has been going on for donkey's years! [*Aggressively*] My Mother feared you. Feared and loathed you, Bricks! You have haunted our lives, your shadow cast itself across our childhood hours – you, you made my Mother do mad things, and destroyed my Father's health – [*with venom*] you! You lie, you cheat, and you destroy! [*Scornful*] To think my Mother actually feared you – you! A puffed up pathetic creature that has crawled at my feet. [*Triumphantly*] A creature who is universally reviled as The Reptile at The Ritz –!

[*The candles flicker and become dim.*

Fay *in shadow.*

Billy *is lit.*]

Billy: [*The beautiful voice*] Am I not admired? [*Abruptly*] Am I not admired as the perfect epitome of the perfumèd gentleman? My dress, my very coiffure, are they not the sacred esthètique at the heart of the temple of my toilette? [*Beat*] Am I not adored? Am I not adored as the universal debonair friend? [*2 beats abruptly. An elegiac tone*] A blind behavioural beast ... am I? A poor creature who experiences flashes, brief illuminations of a grandiose higher self? A courtly, eloquent superior being, who struts the globe with ease? Elegant, eloquent with perfect repose...? Or do I suffer the illusion that I am a fragrant confection of civilisation itself? [*Beat*] Without equal? [*Beat*] Without peer? And quintessentially of a higher more perfect self? [*Beat*] Indeed, in all actuality the magnification of the gentle self, soul? And yes, that of a rare and precious pearl cultivated in an eclectic landscape of sweet music, poetry and hermetic philosophy ... is it not true? [*With righteous indignation*] And was I not walked hand in noble hand amongst the Harmony of the Spheres, according to the Hermetic Gafurius? [*Beat. Firmly*] 'De harmonia musicorum instrumentorum'. And – yes, with a novel Vico twist, by the sylphlike, enchanted birdsong of a Siren – dear, dearest Mother ... alas. She suffered so, amongst the ruins of nature's souvenirs. [*2 beats. Darkly*] Or do I sense the echo of a ferocious creature? A creature who eats up his victims to the bone? An anthropological enormity who lives and feeds amongst the gentle folk? A kind of half-formed beast in eternal flux? [*Beat*] Me? I? [**Billy** *glances over at* **Fay**] Truth, lies or fancy in diabolic loop? A volatile creature – me? I? [*Beat*] Or is this the mad machinations of a pathologically obsessed girl dreamed up in the fires of some maternal frustration against a gentle innocent darkly imagined in an infernal reel of knife twisting ... truth or lies? The Ritz? The Ritz? [*Beat*] The ghostly Ritz ... was I a monstrous Punch who conspired in whispers under its crystal chandeliers? And who laid poison at the heart of its hallowed eating hall? [*Abruptly*] And would I hide the sun to confuse the moon – certainly not! Not I! [*Beat*] Am I not a builder of cities in the noble tradition of Apollodorus – surely not I? [*He studies the room. Pause. Suspiciously*] Can it be that I am spellbound by some mischievous force that has so decided to conjure-up this, this wedding cake, this table, this chair, this girl? [*2 beats*] And if so, is she my judge, my gaoler over of some mysterious crime? [*Beat*] Or is she merely a chess piece in some greater game? [*Beat*] Or indeed is she herself the architect of this strange business? [*2 beats*] A ghost? A ghost? [*He looks with great caution at her*] A ghost? [*Fearful*] Elizabeth ... can it be? [**Billy** *looks nervously about the room. He sighs, he relaxes*] Or is it the room, the room itself that has invented this hallucination, and induced this girl, this phantom up into a capricious dream ...? [**Billy** *looks hard and long at her. Abrupt. A melancholy tone*] No. [*Beat*] My swan hath woven her own dark spell:

> Fantôme qu'à ce lieu son pur éclat assigne,
> Il s'immobilise au songe froid de mépris
> Que vêt parmi l'exil inutile le Cygne.[9]

> *Slow Fade*

---

[9] See references at end

10

Another part of the wood.

Freddie *is sitting in a tree, and peering into the night. while* **Dido** *stands below watching him.*

Dido:	Well! [*Beat*] Anything?
Freddie:	It really is ...
Dido:	What? [*Beat*] What is?
Freddie:	It's bathed in moonlight –
Dido:	W-What is?
Freddie:	[*To himself*] FFFFuck –!
Dido:	What is!
Freddie:	The castle! [*Amazed*] The little bastard really does have a castle –
Dido:	What's –
Freddie:	Shhhhh –!
Dido:	Wh –
Freddie:	Shhhhh! Something is happening –
Dido:	Wh-What is –?
Freddie:	Shhhhh!
	[*A long pause*]
	F, F, F, FUCK –!
Dido:	Wh – What is happening –?
Freddie:	Shhhh! Unbelievable ... it's the vegetation ... it's actually climbing up its walls ...
Dido:	[*Carefully*] Are you on anything?
	[*Silence*]
	[*Gently*] Have you recently taken any medication?

[Silence

Freddie *suddenly stares down at* **Dido***.*

2 beats

And then continues to peer into the night.

Pause]

Dido: [*With a degree of optimism*] Then it's an optical illusion!

[*2 beats*]

Freddie: Not from up here it's not. And we're really very, very close.

Dido: [*Tentatively, looking about*] Moonlight and shadow … [*To herself*] It's this blasted wood! It's full of moonlight and shadow. [*Objectively*] Now, now there's supposed to be a body of water – yes …? Can you see it, anything?

Freddie: And I'm telling you there's an awful lot of nature creeping up its walls – and no. Nothing from this side. But there's a path ahead, and it's very busy with some very serious green stuff indeed … rather iffy I'd say.

[*A rogue wind briefly rustles some leaves.*]

Dido: [*Spooked*] Have you happened to notice, that the closer we appear to get to our destination, so the wilder the foliage appears to have become?

Freddie: No. Not at all. [*With irony*] Because it's only an optical illusion, after all – [*looking down at* **Dido**] fucking right! This place is weird and it's schizophrenic, and it frightens the shit out of me!

[*He slips, but regains his balance. Looking about.*]

Yeah, even the leaves look like they've just grown teeth – but of course it's only moonlight and shadow –

[*He slips again regaining his balance with some difficulty.*]

Dido: [*Looking about*] You had better come down before you fall down.

[*With some reluctance he clambers down awkwardly.*

Both *step away from the tree together.* **Dido** *stops suddenly, and goes to speak, as a moth flutters above her head.* **Both** *watch transfixed, as it slowly settles on her nose.*]

[*Whispered*] The Rannech Sprancher –

Freddie: [*Involuntarily*] Brachionycha Nubeculose.

Dido: [*Quite still, in whispered astonishment*] You! You have remembered!

[*The moth flutters away into the night.*]

[*With great excitement*] You have remembered! [**Freddie** *appears confused, and disoriented. Gently*] You. Before all our ups and downs – you, the golden half of a golden child. The scholar, the scientist, the adventurer, the debonair dashing fellow about town. [*Beat. With nervous expectation*] Do you remember how I snoozed at your feet, as you typed out your dazzling paper for The Zoological Society, 'On the beneficial toilet arrangement between the Borneo mountain shrew, and the Nepenthes Rajah'? [*Jubilantly*] The poo-eating pitcher plant! [*With great warmth*] Dear Doctor, welcome back to the real world!

Freddie: [*A haunted tone*] I, I … can't …?

[*Hunters with dogs are heard.*]

Banjo: [*Up close, and thunderous*] Fee, fie, foh fum, I smell di blood of an Englishman. [*Beat. Thunderous laughter*]

[**Freddie** *and* **Dido** *cower together.*]

[*Mischievously*] BoBo mi come to play. [*Thunderous laughter*] Hey! 'Member di happy time in mi magic parlour puzzle ...? Yeah, too much bad dream for little Freddie, eh? [*Warmly*] Come. Be hugged by di BoBo, and look into mi big green eye ... [*Thunderous laughter*] come! Come close to di BoBo.

[**Freddie** *and* **Dido** *crumble to the ground together.*]

[*Slyly*] BoBo he got di sweeties for little Freddie, yeah?

[*They do not move.*]

[*Abrupt, and commanding*] Come! Di sweetie shop now open for di business.

[*They do not move.*]

[*Soft and teasing*] Tut, tut. No dreamy time for little Freddie?

[*2 beats

Both *crawl frantically into a bush.*]

[*Thunderous laughter. And with great benevolence*] Come. Yu safe now. Yu make old bones wid di BoBo.

[*The bush trembles.*]

[*Sharply, business like*] Come! No worries, no cuss-cuss, no Coocoomaccastick... [*Gently*] easy time ... lazzzee.

[*The bush trembles.*]

[*Darkly*] BoBo, he got di big cat eye for Freddie – [*Playfully*] I sees yu – under mi chinny, chin, chin ...

[*The bush trembles violently.*]

[*With menace*] BoBo jump, BoBo leap, BoBo creepy, creep. [*Impishly*] I'll purr thee to sleep Freddieeee....

[*The beautiful voice, whispered*]: I sometimes conceal my tracks from all humankind ...

It echoes majestically.

Ic swape hwilum

Mine bemipe monna gehwylcum –![10]

[*The tiger roars. The hippos bellow. The bush trembles. Silence. Stillness. The tiger roars. The hippo's duet. The bush trembles. Brief silence. Stillness. A chorus of wild and domestic animals are heard. The bush trembles. Silence. Stillness. The tiger and the hippos trio. The bush trembles. Silence. Stillness. The bush shakes violently with heated whispers. An owl is heard to hoot. Abrupt silence. Stillness. The owl is heard to hoot. A duck is heard to quack. The bush shakes violently with heated whispers. The tiger roars. Silence. Stillness.*

Fade Out

---

[10] See references at end

11

The Room.

Billy *and* **Fay** *are now together on the couch.*

Fay *lies asleep, her head rests in* **Billy***'s lap.*

Both *are in shadow.*

Billy: [*The beautiful voice*] Sleep now, and allow our little world to wrap you up in its dream. Wars may come and go, and generations may be lost, and cities may rise in the deserts, and fall into the seas ... fear not. We will sleep on safe and sure in our little earthCradle. And in the morning when we awaken, and brush aside The Sleep, and go down our winding steps, with care amongst the roots and weeds, and step carefully out into our garden amongst the tulip and thyme, and in the stillness of the hour, we will pause in our bower of hyacinth and wild lilac, before stepping tiptoe in hush around our waking-

[*The candles flicker, and the room transforms into a woodland scene.*

voice-over]

bees, in beech and witch hazel.

And we will make our way down the gravel drive, and pass slowly through those hornèd gates,[11] and up and along the acorn path, and over the little red bridge, and pass under the gallows, watched over by its three

[**Freddie** *appears naked and suspended from a tree by his wrists. His head and body are shaven, and marked in mystical signs.*

He stares down at **Dido***, who stands attentive. When the*

_____
11 See references at end

black ravens. And pass silently past our grazing sheep, and in through the little church gate. [*Fade in, faintly, the toll of a bell*] To pause, and reflect before our waiting tomb and slowly out, and on to the Village Green, between the Stocks and the Bofor's gun. And we will sit and wait and greet our sleepy village folk, and lead them up the old woodland path [*Fade out bell*] and on, and into the shadow of the great tree. And there together, each in our own silent, sombre way, we will gather up our brother's bones, and take them down to the water's edge, and cleanse them in the waters, and place them in our little boat, and push our little boats, and set our little sails, to blow our little boats, around the shore, and up the bend of the river, watched over by the hippos, the herons, and the swans, and yes, the kingfisher, too ... yes, up the bend of the river towards The Devil's Door –

death rattle is heard, **Dido** *slowly returns to the nature and posture of a dog. She sniffs the ground and moves about in a highly confused manner, stopping abruptly to stare out into the darkness, she returns to sit and stare up at the body. She whimpers, she howls and briefly stares out into the darkness again, before leaving her scent against the tree, and disappearing into the night.*]

Blackout

Silence

A thunderclap

Dark. A thunderous sky. Pause. Thunder and lightning. It rumbles away. Pause. First light. 2 beats. A cock is heard to call. Pause. Fade up on a vast blue sky. And fade in the sound of bubbling water, birds and bees. The tiger roars. Beat. The tiger roars. Beat. The hippos bellow. Pause. The tiger roars. Beat. The hippos duet. Beat. The tiger and the hippos trio. Fade out. Pause. Vapour is seen to rise up and form into a small cloud. Beat. And BoBo's laughter is heard to echo in the valley, together with soft rural sounds, and the drifting smell of pine. Fade out natural sounds, and fade in vibrant pastoral music.

The music fades.

Fay *Voice-over. Sleepily:* Sunrise illuminates our little world …

A parrot is heard to screech:

Wi O' Kum! Wi O'Kum! Wi O'kum!

It echoes.

The sun has risen.

Vallis Vocant
DJD

Notes

1
Francis A. Yates, *The Art of Memory*. Routledge and Kegan Paul.

2
Franciso López de Gómara, *Historia de la Conquista de Mexico*. Translated by Yuval Noah Harari, with John Purcell and Haim Watzan.

3
Henrik Ibsen. *Peer Gynt*. ABE Books. *Round and about*.

4
Charles Dickens, *A Christmas Carol*, Chapter 3, 2 of the spirits: ... *(ignorance)* and want.

5
T.S. Elliot, *The Wasteland*. *II*. A Game of Chess. The *(Chair)* she *(sat in)*, like a burnished *(throne)*.

6
Pico della Mirandola, *On the Dignity of Man*: who would not *(admire)* this chameleon? Translated by Edgar Wind.

7
Ovid, *Fasti* V. 194: ... while from her lips she vernal roses breathed. Translated by John Evelyn.

8
A.A. Milne, *When We Were Very Young*. Market Square.

9
Stéphane Mallarmé, *A Faun's Afternoon*, Ecloque,
The Faun:
A phantom condemned to this place by his pure brilliance, he stays motionless in the cold dream of scorn worn in his useless exile by the Swan.

10
The Exeter Riddle Book, Translated by Kevin Crossley-Holland.

11
Odyssey, *XIXI*, 562-7.
Aeneid, *VI*, 893-6.

12
Acknowledgement
Understanding Jamaican Patois
L. Emilie Adams